Praise for *M*

"From the pen of a young indian writer, this is a ... novel about consumerism, and more. It talks about solitude, sex and the role each of us play in society. And it hides all this in a wonderful world of clothes, handbags and high heels." *Elle* (Italy)

"A fascinating book on the seductive (and toxic) power of shopping. Stronger than the pang of conscience we suffer every time we hand our credit card over with a smile to the shop assistant." *Marie Claire* (Italy)

"A first-person tale, intimate and incisive, carefree and disturbing." *Femina* (France)

"[*My Beautiful Shadow*] is a fascinating and dangerous novel. Very much like display windows, it knows how to attract us to make us fall into its trap." *Page* (France)

"An acerbic critic of the cult of beauty and luxury, the author presents an unexpected portait of Japan that is nothing like we imagined." *Lire Supplément* (France)

"An intimate and incisive, carefree and disturbing first-person tale." *Femina* (France)

"Radhika Jha describes perfectly the lack of self confidence that can lead to robotic and destructive addiction." *Telerama* (France)

My Beautiful Shadow

Radhika Jha

JACARANDA

This edition first published in Great Britain 2017 by
Jacaranda Books Art Music Ltd
Unit 304 Metal Box Factory
30 Great Guildford Street,
London SE1 0HS
www.jacarandabooksartmusic.co.uk

First published in India in 2014 by Fourth Estate
An imprint of HarperCollins Publishers India

A CIP catalogue record for this book is available from the British
Library

ISBN: 978-1-909762-47-3
eISBN: 978-1-909762-48-0

Printed and bound in India
by Imprint Press, Rickmansworth, WD3 8RQ

Part One

My Beautiful Shadow

I have a secret. I belong to a club. You can see its members everywhere, in Ginza, in Marounouchi, in Aoyama and Omotesando—all the very best addresses in town. It is a very big club, easily the biggest in Tokyo, in Japan, maybe in all the world. But it is not a famous club. You don't have to fill any forms to join it. It doesn't have a dress code or a rule book. Not even a name. It also has no entrance or membership fees, though the expenses you might incur to remain a member would dwarf the fees of the most exclusive Chiba golf club. And there is no age limit for joining. It just takes some time to get accepted.

Actually it is the club that is secret. It is secret in the sense that its members do not know each other. We see each other. We grow to recognize each other. On occasion we even smile at each other. But we do not try to know each other. That is one of the unwritten rules.

Belonging to a club is different from belonging to a group. Everyone is born into a group. You are a man and I am a woman. You are American and I am Japanese. We did not decide this. It was decided for us. We were not given a choice.

Joining a club, however, is like entering a love marriage, for here we get to choose. That is why we all want to belong to a club. Until we find our club, our spirit is without anchor and so we feel anxious. The longer it takes for us to find our club, the more anxious we get. Then one day we find the club to which we must belong. No longer do we wander aimlessly through life. We have a purpose. And though the line in front of the entrance may be long, we wait patiently, full of that special energy called gaman, forbearance. When the doors of the club open and our name is finally called, we enter it with pride.

There is, however, one restriction on membership to my club: only women may belong. Men say ladies cannot keep a secret. But it is the men who cannot. My club is the biggest, best-kept secret among all of Tokyo's secrets. Many of its own members don't even know that they have joined it.

And my club may not be the oldest of Tokyo's clubs but it is certainly the largest. None of us knows how many members it has. But I see us everywhere—in the metro, in the streets, in the banks and government offices, and the hospitals. How then, you might ask, do we recognize each other? I cannot speak for the others but I have a gift. I can recognize my sister members at a glance. And they acknowledge me sometimes with a small knowing smile or just a raised eyebrow.

Had I been someone else I might have tried to make money with this knowledge. Banks or credit card companies would have paid me millions for what I know. But I do nothing with it, for my club's members are my sisters. I know their habits. I know what they are thinking at 6 p.m. on a Sunday evening as they prepare the family dinner. Or at 11 a.m. on a Monday morning when they are strolling down the main avenue of Ginza, waiting for the shopgirls to welcome them inside. And I know what they feel when at 3 p.m. on a Tuesday afternoon in Marounouchi, they walk with bowed head and hurried, guilty steps towards the metro. My heart fills with pride when I see the pretty ones—so tall and slim and beautiful, their silhouettes ageless. But it is the bravery of those who are tired and old but continue to want to remain young that moves me to tears. What humiliations must they have suffered to remain so long in the club!

Like all clubs, my club has its factions, and its politics. There are two main opposing groups in my club—the housewives and the office ladies. The former have time but little money to spend. They go to the shops and they look and look and look before they buy. They bribe the sales staff to get invited to the family sales. They are so imaginative, so creative and the results of their hard work is so elegant that I cannot help feeling proud of them.

The office ladies have money, but no time. They work alongside men in their offices from nine in the morning till eight or nine at night, only going shopping on weekends and during lunch breaks or after work sometimes if they are lucky enough to finish before the shops close. They complain a lot, the way younger sisters do. They say that we wives are lucky, we get the best buys while they, coming later, must content themselves with what remains. That is why they claim they aren't as well-dressed as we are. The truth, however, lies somewhere else. Actually these women are little girls. They don't want to grow up, they cannot cook. They buy a lot of rubbish—frilly dresses and flowery blouses. Flowers decorate their bags and scarves too. And they love to accessorize. Computers and mobile telephones glitter, keys jangle and even their nails are encrusted with jewels. They like to think that they can steal the love of our men. But they are wrong. Our men are already sold. The company has their love. The only place they have left for an office lady is in their ego. If she knows how to look after it well, she will hold on to him. If not, she will lose him.

There is also a third group of members that belong to neither group and is despised by both—the housewives that dress like office ladies. The women of this group are such skilled actresses and their desire burns so strongly within them that even their bodies look young and virginal. But it is an illusion. The fact that they are in the shops at 11 a.m. and 3 p.m., times when real office girls are working, betrays them. The men know it too, and their eyes quicken when they see them. And indeed they deserve to be admired. For nothing in their look is left to chance—from their long shiny nails and carefully set, glistening hair, to their Hermes scarves and Louis Vuitton bags. And what combinations of colour—purple and orange, lilac and brown, grey and ice blue. These are not invented between the pages of a fashion magazine. They are conjured up by my sisters and worn bravely on the streets of Tokyo. When I stroll around Ginza or Minami Aoyama I never feel alone; for I am surrounded by my sisters and can walk with pride.

You can call my club the beauty lovers club. But we aren't lovers of someone else's beauty. We do not chase beautiful things, or fill our homes with pretty, useless stuff. We don't walk miles to see a beautiful view or a rare bird or pay ridiculous prices to hear what foreigners call "beautiful" music. This is because we do not covet beauty created by others. We want to create our own kind of beauty and do it on ourselves. And the beauty we make is not static or passive, for we make and remake it every day. We are the true aesthetes, for we carry our beauty on our bodies. And even if our homes are old and crumbling, and the walls stink of old age and weariness, when we step outside after our morning toilet, we are young, fresh and gorgeous. And our clothes and make-up are perfect.

A Good Man

Perhaps you have already guessed to which group I belong. Yes, I belong to the married ladies group. Are you surprised? Listen to my story and you will understand.

I married at seventeen and I was proud to be married. For I was not pretty like my friend Tomoko Ohara. There was no part of Tomoko that was not perfect. Her ears were small and well-shaped and sat flat against the side of her head. She was tall and slim like a model. Her skin was fine and translucent, and seemed to glow with the kind of pale blue light that belonged only to the finest Chinese porcelain. But beauty, like a candle flame, creates dark shadows where it goes. Tomoko had only to walk into a room for all other girls to feel that they had ceased to exist. No girl wanted to live in Tomoko's shadow. So she chose me to be her friend. I knew I was never going to be beautiful. But when I was with Tomoko, the world would become a brighter place.

And what did I look like, you ask?

No. I won't embarrass myself by telling you how I looked then. Let me just say that from middle school onwards I felt I had these pumpkins on my chest. Though we had once been quite rich, by the time I was in middle school, all my mother could afford to buy was second-hand clothes and only a few of them ever fit me properly—especially on the chest. The only new clothes I ever got were uniforms—a winter and a summer one. But even there my mother would cheat, buying me only two white shirts instead of three, so that when a classmate threw indelible ink on one of them, I had to wear a sweater in summer to hide the spots.

It was thanks to Tomoko that I met my husband.

When it came to boyfriends, Tomoko could have had any of the boys in Gyosei, the elite boys school just around the corner from ours. Most girls in our school dreamed of marrying a Gyosei boy and many did. But Tomoko didn't want any of them. She wanted someone older, more mature—a man. So from middle school onwards she hunted college students. And that is how I found myself going out with a college boy when I was only in the third year of high school.

Ryu Nishikawa was the best friend of Yasuo, Tomoko's boyfriend-at-the-time. He was a scholarship boy from Kita-Kyushu at the southern end of Japan, and lived in a dormitory for Kyushu students near Yotsuya station run by the Christian priests. Tall, dark skinned and thin, so thin that his elbows seemed on the verge of making holes in his shirts, Ryu's physical appearance was the exact opposite of me. I was short and a little plump, and my skin, like that of most city girls, was pale, almost white.

The first time we met he did not say a word but I caught him staring at my breasts several times. I too found myself staring at him. He reminded me of a bird, he was so brown and silent. But his eyes were really bright and hungry and when he looked at me I felt warm, as if I were sitting in the spring sunshine. So I wasn't really surprised when Tomoko told me he wanted to see me again. Tomoko loved things that tied up neatly and so my going out with her boyfriend's best friend thrilled her. "This way we will always be together," she giggled, giving me the news. "We can go on double dates and go to movies and restaurants together. Isn't that just perfect?" Of course it was. In my grey world, being with Tomoko was the best thing I could imagine in life. But I was worried too. For how could I hold a college man's interest? I was not beautiful or clever or well-dressed like Tomoko. Nor did I have a rich and successful father.

Tomoko solved this problem for me too. The second time Ryu and I met, it was for a movie, and I was wearing a black velvet blouse that Tomoko had lent me. The deeply scooped neckline surrounded by old-fashioned cream lace highlighted the whiteness of my breasts and the deep valley between them. We matched the blouse with a plaid Burberry skirt, also Tomoko's, in rich tones of brown, beige and burgundy. The skirt was very short, which I hoped would compensate for the shortness of my legs, especially when compared to Tomoko's. I had stolen money from the emergency box at home and had my hair and make-up done at Damm, the most popular beauty parlour in Harajuku. It was the only time I ever stole from my mother and she must have noticed, but she never spoke to me about it.

During the movie he kept turning his head to look at me and afterwards offered to escort me to the metro station. He got straight to the point the moment the other two were out of sight, grabbing my breasts and pushing me against the rough trunk of a cherry tree. Though I eventually managed to push him away, I was surprised at how strong he was.

"*Mada dame!*" I hissed at him. Not now. Then, after I'd straightened and tidied myself up a bit, I said, "I want to see where you live. Can you take me there?"

"Women aren't allowed," he said sulkily, but I could see that he was relieved I hadn't told him to get lost.

"That's all right. I just want to see what it looks like," I replied boldly, "so I can picture you sleeping inside."

So, instead of going our separate ways, we got out of the metro together and walked down to Yotsuya. We walked in silence past the station and alongside Sophia university. The road was lined with cherry trees that were heavy with blossom. As we crossed the bridge we passed a baseball field on our left belonging to Sophia University. Suddenly I stopped. The gate on the side was wide open, someone had forgotten to lock it. I pulled his hand. "Let's go inside."

"Why?" he asked, looking startled.

"Because." I could not tell him that this was the first time I was alone with a man and I was so happy that the happiness bubbling in my blood was making me want to do something different, something that would make me remember this night.

So instead of answering, I just walked inside. I didn't look back, even though he called out my name twice. When I got to the middle of the field which was in semi-darkness, I turned around. And then, I don't know what made me do it, but I took off my blouse.

"What are you doing?" he called. "People will see you."

"Oh really? Then maybe you better come here and put my shirt back on for me," I replied boldly.

So he came. Hesitantly at first, then, his eyes fixed upon my breasts, faster and faster. When he was almost touching distance I turned and ran. "Hey!" he called, running after me. "Wait."

But I didn't wait. I ran straight towards the lone light at the far end of the field. It was one of those old-fashioned streetlights and gave off a warm golden glow. Because Sophia was a private university it could afford to keep the old streetlights and as I waited for Ryu to catch up I remember wondering what those who could afford to go to universities like Sophia looked like. Panting, Ryu stepped into the circle of light and then I thought no more.

Ryu always says that I made him so crazy all of his final year that it was a wonder he even managed to pass his exams. Every evening that year, Tomoko and I would wait for our men outside the gates of Waseda University and then all four of us would go for a coffee at Jonathan's. Afterwards, my husband-to-be and I would begin the long walk to Yotsuya where I would catch the train to Musashi Koganei where my mother lived. But first we went to the baseball field.

Night had fallen. I would go stand under the lamp. There I would take off my shirt, then my bra, and holding my breasts in my palms, offer them to Ryu. He would walk up to me slowly, taking his time. When he was a foot away he would stop and do nothing but stare. Seeing him hesitate I would grow afraid and would push my breasts up even higher. "That first time, yellow light fell like whisky on your breasts," he wrote me in a letter, "spilling into the pool of darkness at your feet. Your breasts were huge and your nipples were like angry eyes daring me to come closer. I was so overwhelmed I could not move." It was the only love letter he ever sent me. It became a game to see who would take the first step and the space between us in those moments was the most exciting thing I had ever known: for there was nothing in that space, yet it felt as full and as precious as a boatful of gold.

But one night my shadow inserted itself between us. I looked at it in surprise for it was a stranger, long and slim and quite unlike me. Then I smiled for I recognized who it was— Tomoko, but with my breasts! I must have fallen in love with my shadow then, for each night I would wait for it to appear and when it did, I would look at nothing else. Even when Ryu was kissing me, I could not drag my eyes away from my beautiful shadow but would continue to watch it as it merged

9

with his, lost its shape and became the many-limbed monster of our courtship.

All year, like Kabuki actors, we went through the same ritual. Then, in March, Ryu received an invitation for an interview with Mitsubishi bank. I could tell from the way he looked at me that night, proudly, as if he owned me, that he had something important to tell me. When he finally closed the gap and touched me gently, the mask dropped, and I saw the naked joy on his face. I knew something very important had happened but for the moment sharing his happiness was enough. Afterwards, as he walked me to the metro station, he told me all about the interview. Then I too cried out in joy, for at last I knew for sure that his future was indeed as bright as I had dreamed it would be.

I can see from your expression that you think I was naïve. But you don't understand. For us the future is very important. No decent woman will marry a man without a future. And men's futures, well, they are not decided on the spur of the moment in a mere interview. In reality, one of Ryu's college seniors, the son of a senior finance ministry bureaucrat, had recommended him and the company had accepted, not because they knew Ryu but because they liked his senpai. The interview was therefore more like the official meeting of two families before an arranged marriage, theatrical but important. For if, at that moment, someone had taken a dislike to Ryu and had opposed his entrance into the bank, his career would have ended even before it had begun. But they must have thought Ryu was okay at the interview for no-one opposed him. I knew they wouldn't. For Ryu had a special talent—he was so completely ordinary he made no-one nervous.

Just before Ryu graduated, he took me on a holiday to a hot spring in Beppu, Oita Prefecture, for a few days and afterwards to his mother in Kita Kyushu. I told the school I was sick and told my mother that I was going with the school team for a volleyball tournament. Neither suspected the truth. In a way it was our honeymoon, for right after graduation, Ryu began work in the loans division of the Akasaka branch office of Mitsubishi bank. It was 1986. Those were still the good days in Japan, starting salaries were high, companies fought over graduates like my husband.

From the start, Ryu was very clear in his mind about what he wanted to do. He wanted to send money to his mother in Kyushu so that she would not have to work. And he wanted to marry me. When I told her, Tomoko spilt some of her hydrochloric acid on the bench. "Shouldn't you wait a bit?" she asked as we hurriedly cleaned up the mess. "He's the first man you've been with. You should go to college and meet other men, then decide what you want." I looked at Tomoko and the gap between us suddenly seemed huge. Tomoko could afford to wait. Meeting men was easy for her. But I knew that if I made Ryu wait he would find someone prettier and smarter than I. The world is filled with beautiful women. Just like it is filled with beautiful flowers. All I had were two grapefruit-sized breasts. I had to be realistic.

My wedding was full of flowers. Everyone from Ryu's office sent a bouquet even though I didn't even know them. Some were huge and even the smallest one must have cost at least fifteen thousand yen! My wedding dress cost less than the flowers. It was a hired one. But what hurt most was that the wedding kimono I wore that morning when we went to the shrine was rented too. This was because my mother was opposed to the marriage. She told me she wasn't going to spend money on a marriage that she felt was a mistake. If my brother had still been living at home maybe he would have taken my side and talked her around. But he was already far away, in America. So Ryu and I waited till I finished school and we got married anyway.

"The white wedding kimono is a very special thing, it is a symbol of marriage itself," my mother would always tell me when she aired out her own at the beginning of spring. Even though nowadays all young girls hire them and spend most of their money on the Western-style wedding dress for the party, my mother was old-fashioned enough to want to dress her daughter in a really beautiful brand-new wedding kimono. "It has to be new," she would explain, "otherwise how will the bride feel special?" My wedding kimono smelled of mothballs—the kind I particularly hated that made you feel instantly old and unappreciated, as if you had been locked away in a cupboard. But marriage is a cupboard into which you are locked for the rest of your life; so actually my kimono was the right one to wear for it gave me a true picture of the life I was entering. Those rich girls with their million-yen kimonos and doting parents are fools! If I had known it then, perhaps I would not have jumped into the marriage so quickly. Perhaps I would have waited, gone to university and looked for something else to do with my life.

But Ryu proposed to me right after he got his appointment letter and I finished school with a ring on my finger. I was the first woman in my class to get one. Imagine that, ordinary me, the first in the class to have an engagement ring. Only Tomoko looked at me and shook her head. I graduated from high school without studying for my exams but passed anyway. For word had got around that I was to marry right after graduation and no-one failed a "soon-to-be-married" girl.

After the wedding we moved into a two-room apartment above a Korean beauty and massage parlour in Okubo. It was a tiny place, with a bedroom no bigger than a cupboard and a kitchen that was shared by us and the Korean girls working downstairs. But they were very kind and we quickly became friends. The Korean girls at the parlour told me how lucky I was to be married. They gave me free samples of Korean beauty products and advice on how to treat a man. Ryu gave me his salary each month and told me to keep it carefully. I felt on top of the world.

Life settled into a routine. My eyes would open as they always had at a quarter to six in the morning. But instead of going to school I went into the kitchen and prepared the bento for my husband's office lunch. I made him the bentos I wished my mother had prepared for me, taking real pains over the cutting of the vegetables, and making sure the food was different each day. After I finished I would return to bed where my husband would be waiting for me.

"You smell like food," he'd say, "I think I'd better eat you."

And we would begin. The bed became our life-raft and we travelled unknown seas together. Everything was new, and like no two waves are ever the same, it was always different.

After Ryu left for work I would remain in bed and enjoy my tiredness. At around eleven I would go downstairs for a shower in the common bathroom and then after getting dressed I'd walk over to Shinjuku and have a coffee while reading the beauty magazines for free. Then, around lunchtime, I'd stop at the grocery store and buy myself a pre-prepared lunch and something for dinner and then I'd sleep a little, watch television or go downstairs and chat with the Korean girls till Ryu came home. After the restrictions of school and the responsibilities of my mother's home, I felt I had arrived in heaven. My favourite fantasy in those days was accidentally meeting Tomoko again. "How is married life?" she'd ask. And

I would tell her just how wonderful it was, how gentle Ryu was with me and how well he was doing at the bank. I imagined her face filling with regret and not a little jealousy.

Then Ryu got promoted. Office parties and dinners for clients became more frequent. He would come home drunk and oversleep so we couldn't have sex in the mornings. I grew tired of being alone so I took a job in a dentist's office in the Bancho area. The work involved taking the phone, making appointments, showing patients where to wait and receiving their payments. It was not hard, and I enjoyed watching the endless stream of rich people. After a few weeks, even though I still made mistakes, the dentist doubled my salary and made me his assistant.

Sometimes Ryu would join me for lunch in the dentist's office but instead of eating we'd lock the door and play dentist with our clothes off. Afterwards, during the afternoon sessions, while helping hold down a frightened patient, I would go into silent convulsions remembering what Ryu and I had done in that very same chair. Sometimes I would shake so hard I made the dentist's hand shake and he would glare at me over his mask, his eyes promising retribution. But he never threw me out. An assistant with big breasts was too much of a prize. Instead, he would lean into me while reaching for an instrument, deliberately touching my breasts with his forearms. So I would glare at him until he was forced to look away. But I didn't leave—for I could not bear the idea of those endless hours in my empty apartment. And when I got my first salary I didn't care even when his careless hands brushed my breasts.

Thus, a new routine began which suited us both. We left for work in the mornings together. Instead of sex we ate breakfast. In the evenings I was so tired that all I could do was sleep in front of the television until Ryu arrived. He would bring home food or if he came early enough we would go out to an izakaya and return home pleasantly drunk. Those were the happiest days of my life. Our marriage was a magic boat. Nothing could overturn it.

But in 1988, two years after we married, I had to leave the dentist's office. Not because he found someone prettier and easier to bend over his dentist's chair, but because I became pregnant. In our culture, a pregnant woman is an ugly woman. If you cannot hide what a man has done to you, you must hide yourself. That is virtually a rule. To walk the streets with an ugly bulge is to occupy someone else's potential space. That is also rude. So, when it was no longer possible to hide my bulge politely behind my white lab coat, I quit. My husband however got promoted when he told his boss that his wife was pregnant. Three months before the baby arrived we moved out of our tiny apartment above the Korean massage shop in Okubo and into a proper four-room house on the edge of Setagaya ward. The house wasn't ours, it belonged to the bank. Downstairs there was a kitchen and a small tatami-covered sitting-cum-dining area which could also be used as a guest bedroom. A tiny toilet was tucked under the wooden stairs which led up to the second floor. Up the narrow stairs were the two bedrooms, one in the back, one in the front. I sat at home, hiding myself and waiting for an unknown creature to stop inhabiting my body.

Eventually the baby came out and it was a boy. Being a mother made everything worse. Now I had two creatures that suckled my breasts till they were raw. To add insult to injury, my breasts grew so huge I could not find anything to wear. So I had to sew myself a few dresses and since I didn't know how to sew very well, the dresses hung so poorly that I dared not go

15

out in them. The baby grew quickly. It drank and drank and drank without stopping and then at night just as the baby and I fell asleep out of sheer exhaustion, my husband came home demanding food and sex and then he would suckle my breasts till he fell asleep. "I can only sleep on your breasts," he would tell me, "they are the best pillows in the world." I could not sleep for I had no pillow.

I would look at my breasts and at the round black head of my husband in between them and a queer thought would come to me: my breasts were aliens, they did not belong to me. They occupied the air in front of me, they used me for nourishment. I was the ground from which they had sprouted, that's all. They were alien beings that had come in the night from a spaceship and planted themselves on my chest. And because I had been such a fertile ground, these alien plants had grown big and round, too big and too outspoken for Japan, and so they had to be punished again and again in order for them to learn their place. Because of my breasts I too was being punished. Looking at my breasts and at the head of my husband who so fully enjoyed them, I felt angrier and angrier. It was not a new thought but one that had been waiting in the wings for a long, long time. In the absolute darkness of the night, a great tsunami of anger would crash over my head. But I could not move, I could not save myself—because of the sleeping head of my husband who had to go to work the next day, feeling refreshed.

In the morning the ache in my stone-hard breasts would awaken me before the baby's cries and I would have just enough time to rush to the toilet and empty my bladder before grabbing the child. My husband would wake up and watch sleepily while I fed our son, and with my husband's eyes and my child's mouth sucking away the pain of the previous night, something magical would happen to me. As my breasts grew small and light I was returned to myself and I would smile at my husband and feel at peace with the world.

For a little while.

Two Visitors

Though still within the limits of the city, the new neighbourhood in Setagaya was the opposite of Okubo. Whilst in Okubo there was always noise and the streets were full of passers-by, in our new place there was only silence and the odd car or bicycle. Though the houses were built close together, they did not touch and the curtains remained tightly drawn even on the hottest summer day. And the people behind the curtains rarely showed their faces. Even when they put out the garbage for collection, they did so furtively.

But this did not mean we were not being looked at. From behind the curtained windows, invisible eyes kept track of our comings and goings. Sharp ears listened when we went to the toilet, counting how many times in the night we pulled our flush. And so they quickly learned everything about us—while we remained in ignorance about them.

After the noise of Tokyo, I could not get used to the tranquillity of the new house. It kept me awake at night and I spent the time imagining the sirens of ambulances and the steady hum of traffic, longing for the lights of the city. Sometimes I went to the window, opened it—and saw not a single light other than the street lamps. In Okubo we had to keep our curtains closed tight at night to make an approximation of darkness. In the new house, from morning till evening and from evening till the following morning, the silence, like the darkness, was undisturbed.

Ten months passed from the time I stepped inside that house and I never went outside. Not even once. My husband, who had in the meantime been transferred to the branch in Ikebukuro, one hour and fifteen minutes away from the house by train, left at six-thirty in the morning and returned at ten at night. I ordered milk and groceries over the telephone and every evening my husband would bring home some prepared fish or chicken. I waited inside the house like a giant undersea creature, hungry for noise and visitors. But the visitors never came.

When I fed the baby I was tortured by dirty thoughts. I imagined myself wearing an orange silk kimono lying spread-eagled on the futon, tied up in satin ribbons with a gag in my mouth. I imagined unknown men coming into the house, opening the door and walking up the narrow stairs into the room, looking at me and photographing me. I saw myself as a photo, and got excited thinking of all those unknown men looking at me. Such terrible thoughts went on till the baby had drunk enough. Then I would masturbate and fall asleep.

Six months after my son Akira's birth I discovered an interesting fact. I had lost a lot of weight. I was not yet fashionably thin, but definitely much thinner than I had been. My stomach was no longer rounded and in its place was a set of three wrinkles that flowed like water when I moved. When I was wearing clothes the wrinkles were hidden. On the other hand what did show were my hips and legs—which were slim now, as were my thighs and calves. And nothing that I owned fit me any more. Ryu was the one who made me notice this. "You have lost weight after the baby," he told me approvingly, "you have a nice body now. Go to Tokyo and buy yourself something new, something nice. Make yourself pretty again."

Now I recognize them instantly, those first-time mothers going out with their first-time babies. Everything about them feels like clothes washed once too often. Only the stroller, the shiny McLaren stroller, looks brand new. But I also know that as the year progresses, the McLaren will get that well-washed look too, but the mothers will become brighter and better dressed.

I cannot remember what I wore the first time I went out with Aki-chan. I remember only what I bought that day— for I have it with me still. One day I will sell it to a vintage brand shop, for it still looks almost new. It is the classic brown Louis Vuitton tote, perfect for carrying all that a baby needs— pampers, rattles, creams and bottles.

But that day, as I walked from Omotesando station towards the Harajuku crossing, pushing Akira in front of me in his second-hand stroller, I noticed that all the other young mothers had the same brown shoulder bag with the initials LV printed all over them, hanging off the handles of their McLaren Strollers! Why had I never seen that before? The answer was simple. It was because I hadn't been a mother then. Now, I felt as if I had been given a new pair of eyes that allowed me to see another Tokyo, one I had never seen before—the Tokyo of young mothers. And how fashionable those young mothers were! Perching nonchalantly on impossibly high heels, they were pushing their babies up the avenue in brand-new McLarens, designer sunglasses perched delicately on the tips of their tiny noses. They all had heavily mascaraed eyelashes, wore at least three shades of eye-shadow, sheer lip gloss over their lipstick, and Shiseido's expensive pearl face powder. Their long hair was freshly blow dried to fall away from their faces in glossy waves. Their slim girlish legs were clad in sexy shorts or short, short skirts. Their small, hard, milk-swollen breasts peeped out at the world through filmy chiffon blouses fringed with handmade lace. And around their slim throats they wore gold or pearls, nothing artificial—just discreet married woman jewellery.

When I had set out that morning, using my husband's belt to hold up my jeans, I had felt slim and full of hope. But when I saw them I felt ugly again. My hair had not seen a hairdresser in a year, my clothes were too big, and my nails were unpolished.

I walked up and down the avenue twice trying to decide which shop to enter. I didn't think I was smart enough to enter any shop but my husband's credit card, heavy and hot in my pocket, reassured me. I put my hand inside and held on to it so tight that the raised initials of my husband's family name burned themselves into my palm. Then, as I was about to pass the front of the Louis Vuitton store for the third time, I entered. I am not sure but the price of the brown-and-beige leather tote bag with the Louis Vuitton initials must have been around 200,000 yen. It was the first time I used my husband's card. I didn't know how it worked and was scared to reveal my ignorance. But the shopgirl was very kind. She took the card and came back with a slip of paper. "Sign here please," she said, showing me where I must put my mark. It was so simple. Then she gave me the bag and the receipt and it was mine. I walked out proudly with the bag hanging off the side of my second-hand McLaren. As I left the shop, the shopgirls chorused "*Arigatoogozaimashita*" and I felt like a queen. The sun was setting as I walked towards Harajuku station. I noticed my shadow had become that of a manga girl, sinuous and curvy. I felt a part of them then, those glamorous mothers with the long brown hair and high heels. I looked down at my baby and smiled at him fondly. And when the men turned to look at me I felt good.

But the feeling didn't last long. When I got back to the house, depression descended upon me. A horrid smell assailed my nostrils and I realised that Aki-chan had done a huge potty. It was as if I was being punished for my selfishness for I was once more up to my elbows in filth and bad smells. Then, just as I finished cleaning the baby, my breasts began to call out, demanding relief. I wrapped Akira in a towel, sat down in a chair by the kitchen table, and shoved his face onto my aching breast. Even before his mouth got a grip on the nipple, the milk came pouring out, wetting my shirt and dribbling down my body.

That day, maybe because I had been happy, my breasts were like live volcanoes. Even Aki-chan could barely keep up. Through the kitchen door I could see the stroller waiting in the hallway. I noticed a brown spot on the seat and frowned. It would have to be cleaned too. Then my eyes fell on the Louis Vuitton bag, still hanging from the handle of the McLaren. And suddenly, more real than a dream, more real than the house I was in, I saw myself floating down Omotesando again, free and powerful, a glamorous, beautiful mama, respected and lusted after at the same time. Fantasy had replaced memory, so that I was dressed like them in flowing tops and shorts and high, high heels. Like a detective who at last sees the face of a criminal he has been hunting a long time on a shop surveillance video, I stopped the video tape in my head and let the camera zoom into a close-up of their sandals. I wanted some exactly like those, strapped around the ankles with colourful tassels hanging off the back. Desire flooded my body, so strong it felt real, like the warm salty milk draining out of my breasts. Aki-chan was almost asleep now. The towel I had wrapped him in was wet. He had urinated on it as he

23

drank. Suddenly I couldn't bear the combined smell of milk and urine any more and, putting the baby in his cot, I ran into the bathroom for a shower.

But of course I had forgotten to burp the baby and just as I was thoroughly wet, Akira began to howl. I let him cry. It felt good to make him suffer. Then, when it got louder and angrier, I realised that the neighbours would arrive and wrapping a towel around me quickly I rushed out and grabbed the baby.

The next day I had two visitors. The first came around nine-thirty in the morning when I had just slipped into a light sleep. Akira was playing with his toys on the bed beside me and the house was quiet. The bell shocked both of us. It had a particularly loud, unmusical sound—because like everything else in the house it was cheap. At first I thought it was an earthquake siren. Then it came again and I realised what it was. It was the first time I was hearing it. My husband always used his key.

I wrapped an apron over my pajamas to make it look as if I had been housecleaning and rushed to open the door. The woman on the other side was in her late fifties and her grey hair was tinged purple from the old-fashioned indigo rinse she used. Her clothes were also quite plain, not cheap, just boring. But her feet in their sensible walking sandals were nice, small and slim, ending in well-turned ankles. She had a small package in her hand, nicely tied up in a yellow furoshiki. "*Ojyamashimasu.* Hello. Sorry to disturb you. I am your neighbour. Seki Asako is my name." She smiled furtively, her eyes darting behind me.

I opened the door a little wider and invited her in. I should have been worrying about the state of the house, for I hadn't cleaned yet but instead, felt quite excited. This stranger was my first visitor, the first person I had ever invited into my new house. I felt proud, so proud that I quite forgot to be scared of what she would see. Her eyes darted around curiously as she entered. I think she was a little disappointed that there was so little in the house. They rested briefly on the second-hand stroller, a little longer on the brown spot, and then came back to me.

"You have a baby boy," she said unnecessarily. "Congratulations."

I wondered how she knew we had a boy. "Do you live close by?" I asked curiously.

"*Unhh*, in this street," she answered. "I would have come before but I wasn't sure who lived here. You and your husband were so quiet. It was only..." she ended abruptly, not bothering to finish the sentence.

I realised I had made a mistake. These questions should have been asked after I gave her some tea. So I invited her into the kitchen and made her sit at the yellow Formica table where the night before I had breastfed Aki-chan, and where I usually ate my meals alone. I took out my best tea—a little box of Mariage Frères given to me by Tomoko the last time we met. I untied the furoshiki and placed the fresh sweet potato cakes she had brought on a plate. They looked homemade and my stomach did a somersault in anticipation.

When the tea was ready, I put all of it onto a tray and put it on the table. Then I sat down opposite her and poured some tea in her cup. She bowed her head and waited ceremoniously till I had filled my own cup. During this time I could feel her eyes darting around the kitchen, adding up the cost of the refrigerator and the television, checking for dirt, for signs of untidiness. I was relieved that since we didn't use the living area at all it was quite tidy, and so was the kitchen as I worked in it every day. Then I remembered the pile of dirty clothes in the bathroom and wondered guiltily if I had shut the door properly. We began our conversation.

"These cakes are delicious," I complimented her after taking a small bite.

"Thank you. But I didn't make them. There is a little shop on Heiwa dori. I can take you there if you like."

"I would be very grateful if you could kindly take me there," I answered politely.

We both sipped our tea in silence. "So where were you living before you came to our neighbourhood?" she asked.

"In Okubo," I answered.

"Is that so? With the Koreans." The way she said it made me feel as if I had been living with criminals.

"Yes, rents were low... but I am not Korean," I felt impelled to say.

"I know that," she replied, smiling reassuringly. "You are from Kyushu. Tell me, how are you coping, so young and with a baby?" I was about to reply, ready to pour my lonely heart out. But her next sentence drove what I was going to say straight out of my mind. "Recently we hear it crying quite often," she said, careful not to look at me directly, and all of a sudden I felt naked and dirty.

Why dirty, you ask?

Because shame always makes us feel dirty. I was being shamed by a stranger, a neighbour. There was nothing worse than that.

"I am so sorry," I told her, hanging my head.

"Don't worry." She smiled comfortingly. "We've all had babies. How old is yours?"

"Six months," I replied dully.

"Really? I am surprised. From the way it was crying last night I thought it was older. Strong lungs. That is good. Maybe you can make an opera singer out of him."

I said nothing. I knew I was being punished. Then my neighbour came to the object of her visit. "Garbage," she informed me, looking falsely apologetic. "We have been noticing that you produce a lot of garbage. We don't understand why you should have so much—you are only two people. I thought maybe you weren't aware of these things—you are so young to run your own house and maybe your mother hadn't shown you, so I told the others I would talk to you. You understand—we have to pay more if there is more garbage, taxes go up. So we all have to be careful about how much garbage we make."

This time the shame was even stronger. "I understand. It will not happen again," I said, not looking at her.

Even after I shut the door behind the neighbour I felt watched. Foreigners always ask why Japan is so safe. Why there aren't that many policemen on the road and they never carry guns yet no-one breaks the rules. I will tell you why. It is because of the neighbours. They are your police, your judges and your jailors. But most of all, they are your teachers. What keeps us following the rules is the shame we feel if we are caught disobeying our teachers. And since those who do the catching are also those who do the teaching, this combination of teacher-policeman is inescapable. After Seki-san left, I went and shut the curtains in every room. Still I felt eyes burning holes in my walls. Her voice played endlessly in my ears. I knew then that I was doomed to follow the rules. For I had met my teacher-policeman. And I also realised that from the start I had had no choice in the matter. Marrying against my mother's wishes, which till then had seemed such a free and daring thing to do, living in my own house, mistress of four rooms, all of that was an illusion. I had been wrong from the start. My family was not my teacher-policeman, far from it.

All along it had been her, Seki-san. This was the fate that had awaited me from the beginning. All morning, as I cleaned the house like a demon, I was trembling with rage and yet I couldn't think what to do except submit.

Then the bell rang again. The woman standing impatiently outside my door was roughly the same age as Seki-san but in every other respect she was exactly her opposite. For one thing, she was very fashionably dressed. Nothing in the dress was remarkable in itself but the way it sat on the body, making the wearer seem tall and slim, revealed the genius of the hand that had cut it. In her carefully manicured and painted hands she held a straw-coloured Ferragamo bag with a gold chain and the sandals were brown leather Guccis with pencil-point heels. The subtle scent that clung to her reminded me of irises.

It was my mother.

I took longer letting her in than I had Seki-san. I had not seen my mother since I got married. I didn't want her coming into my new respectable life. My mother had no place in it. She had given up being respectable after my father died. If I could I would have shut my eyes and wished for her to disappear. Instead, I just stared at her stupidly while she tapped one elegantly clad foot impatiently on the paving stone.

"Don't you think you had better ask me inside before your neighbours see me?" she asked sarcastically.

I opened the door a little wider and stepped aside. She came inside and stood in the tiny hallway, struggling to remove her expensive shoes, frowning. But I wouldn't let her keep them on. I watched her struggle and enjoyed it till Akira woke up and, not finding me nearby, began to cry.

By the time I came back downstairs with Akira, she was sitting at the kitchen table where Seki-san had sat, cracking her finger joints.

"So this is my grandchild?" she asked, getting straight to the point.

"Yes, this is Akira, our son," I replied.

"Why didn't you tell me when he was born?"

"Because... there was no time," I mumbled.

"He is not a baby, he is what... six months, eight? A year?" I wished she would leave and my mind began to cast around for ways to disgust her. She looked at the remains of Seki-san's tea lying on the table and said, "So you had visitors already. This early it could only have been the neighbours. You shouldn't let them into your house. You should have pretended you were asleep or not there."

"You should have told me these things earlier," I shot back angrily.

My mother didn't flinch. She just waited for me to finish. Then she said, "You should have told me before the baby was born, I would have helped you. Looking after babies is not easy."

I said nothing, not because I thought she was right but because I felt sure she was lying. She would not have given up her golf and her ikebana and her parties to be with me.

My mother studied me with her cold scientist's eyes. "You've lost weight," she said. "It suits you. Once your breasts deflate a little, you will look very good."

I glared at her, refusing to accept the peace offering.

"Make me some tea," she ordered. "And let's finish these sweet potato cakes. They look good. Where did you buy them?"

"The neighbour brought them, Seki-san."

"You shouldn't let the neighbours inside your house. It will only cause problems," she repeated.

"And if I don't let them in, they will think I am rude," I replied.

My mother sniffed and said nothing. I handed Akira to her and was surprised at how easily she took him onto her lap—

expensive yellow dress and all.

When I came back to the table with the tea, the first thing she said to me was, "I see your husband spoils you. That's good. A nice bag, that Louis Vuitton, if it wasn't so common. Next time get Ferragamo, it is better."

I had opened my mouth to tell her about yesterday's shopping but her last sentence made me stop. The feeling of not being good enough, which she had always inspired, returned. Then, from her lap, Akira reached out for me, tipping over my mother's tea cup. Brown liquid splashed onto my mother's yellow designer dress. She looked at the stain and her face muscles twitched slightly. Calmly, she handed me the baby and walked to the toilet with her handbag. I heard the sound of water and then of a hairdryer. When she emerged ten minutes later there was not the faintest shadow of a mark on her dress. Her make-up was freshly applied. She looked perfect.

And she never came back again.

You must be wondering why am I telling you all this. Maybe you are beginning to wonder if I am lying, if I am making it all up. After all, the woman before you is no spring chicken, isn't that what you English speakers call it? She is around forty, and if you open the blinds there you will see she has the marks of a caesarian on her stomach and her breasts are soft and slightly sagging which is why she keeps her bra on so long. You must think that she cannot possibly remember in such detail such an insignificant event as the purchase of a bag and what happened after. But I can and do remember. I remember every purchase I made—at least the ones I made at the beginning. If I could take you home I could show you the sandals I bought not a day after my mother left. They were Louis Vuitton too. Brown leather, really classic. If I wore them now they would still be elegant. That is what I like about expensive things. They don't fade, they don't change with the sun.

The young girls you see today look fashionable but it is an illusion. For what they wear is cheap and looks cheap as soon as the newness fades. But in the late eighties, Japan was floating in money and we only bought the best. We bought the real luxury. Only from France and Italy. You couldn't get cheap Western things in Japan in those days. Whenever I see my brown leather Louis Vuitton sandals I think of the brown tea splashing onto my mother's dress and how ten minutes later the stain had been washed away. That is Japanese culture for you. We are very good at cleaning up. We also really love beautiful things. My Louis Vuitton sandals, the ones I bought the very next day, will never get wiped away. They cannot be erased with a harsh word like love can. They are mine forever.

Do you want to know why I dislike my mother?

It goes back a long way. Even before my father died, we were not close. And afterwards, when she became our only breadwinner, she was either asleep or not there. My mother, if you haven't already guessed, had become a hostess. For she was still quite young and very beautiful when my father died and well-paid jobs didn't exist for women. So it was the only way she could make enough to send my brother and me to expensive private schools. My mother, being the child of a schoolteacher, was ready to sacrifice everything in order to give her children a good education.

I think the same yakuza who were responsible for killing my father helped her find her first job. But I cannot say for sure as I was too young. All I remember was in the evenings, when we returned from school, the table downstairs was laden with food and my mother was dressing for work upstairs. I took the lids off the plates of lukewarm food and served my brother and myself. We would eat and watch TV and pretend not to notice my mother as she crept down the stairs. I cannot remember a single word she said to me after my father died but I can still remember the clothes she wore. Every little detail.

From the window of the kitchen I would watch her walk down the road till darkness swallowed her. She looked so elegant and free as she walked away from us. I should also mention that the road we lived on was so far from Tokyo that there were no houses there, only fields and behind them, the forest. But that was not what frightened me. It was the way she walked away from us each night, looking so foreign and unlike herself, and the feeling I had each time that maybe she wouldn't come back in the morning.

There's one more thing I must mention. When I was clearing up after my mother left, I found an envelope tucked under her plate. I turned it over curiously, thinking Seki-san had left it for me, for it had my married name on the envelope. Inside was a check for one and a half million yen and a terse note:

Though you have become a mother before you could become a woman, congratulations on your coming-out day. I am sorry I could not give you a proper kimono.

It was signed "your Mother." It was only then that I realised. I had turned twenty.

High Heels

What does a woman do with one and a half million yen? A good woman will deposit the amount in her husband's bank account and use the money for her children's education or for buying them nice clothes so that they look as rich as other children. In short, she uses the money to protect her family from shame. I suppose it began there—as I stared at the cheque in my hand and decided I would not give it to my family but keep it for myself. Perhaps the seeds of my "badness" were always there, planted somewhere inside me and like my breasts, just waiting for the right moment to grow. Instead of depositing the money in my husband's account, I took it and opened an account of my own. I didn't plan on doing anything with the money. If I had a conscious thought, it was that by keeping the money separate, if one day things went bad for my husband the way they had gone bad for my father, I would then be able to produce the money and save him. But maybe that was only what I told myself. For, on the day that I went to open the account, having left Akira in Seki-san's care, when the lady at the bank, a pretty woman with dyed light brown hair and a charming voice, asked me if I wanted a credit card too, I never hesitated, I just said yes. Three weeks later, at twelve-thirty, when I was cleaning up the mess Akira had made while eating in his high chair, the doorbell rang. As usual, it surprised me and I went to the door unprepared. But it was only the postman with a thick letter.

"Sign please," he said, handing me a pen. I signed innocently, thinking it was for my husband. But when I turned the envelope over, the name was mine. I remember how the card shone. It wasn't gold like my husband's, just silver and blue. But I loved it and carefully hid it away, convinced I would never use it.

But of course I used it. My husband was the one who gave me the first push. He told me that buying "Made in Japan" things wasn't good enough for the wife of a rising bank executive. "You should go shopping at least once a month and buy something new, something European," he advised. "And be sure never to be seen without a good handbag. You never know who is watching you."

You say I should leave, that I do not belong here? It is my dream to leave Japan. My best, most favourite dream. Whenever I dream of leaving, the movie I see in my head is that of me entering a green wooden door with a big brass knocker, the kind you see in American movies of the fifties. Three steps lead up from the street to this door. My feet go up these steps. I am wearing a white-and-red summer dress from Dior and my beautiful red Gucci high heels. Though I cannot see it I know I have a Dolce & Gabbana white clutch bag tucked under my left elbow. The dress and the clutch I have with me still. The clutch is my favourite summer bag. You know, I think I made the clutch fashionable in Japan. No-one was carrying them till I got photographed on Omotesando with one. But that is another story. I wish I could show you a photo of me in my twenties so you could see just how glamorous I was. All my husband's colleagues were jealous of him. One of them even said one day when he was drunk that my husband's protector, his senpai from Waseda who got him hired, was in

34

love with me. But that too is another story. Back to my dream. Where was I? Ah yes, the green door. It opens and I enter a sparkling space with a window on either side and no step, no shoes lined up in the hallway. And most of all, no ugly slippers with their silly blunt round noses. I do not bend to remove my sandals, I walk inside my dream house in my high heels which go tip tap, tip tap, tip tap and I enter a big living room with sofas and a beige carpet. My heels sink into the softness of the carpet and I sit on the sofa. A glass of wine appears in my hand and I flip through the pages of a magazine and classical music —Mozart maybe— plays in the background. And all around me there is space and light.

Then I wake up and I am still in Japan and my slippers are sitting beside the bed and my husband is snoring next to me. Heavy red curtains cover the small window and the glass door leading onto our tiny balcony. But this too is a dream—a dream of what used to be. Many years ago my husband exchanged our futons for a Western-style spring mattress. On the mornings when I cleaned the house I put the mattress up against the wall. At other times I left it where it was. When the mattress was down, there was no room for anything else in the room except slippers. I think we should never have exchanged our futons for a spring bed. But my husband was the one who insisted—beds were better for sex, he said. Yet, by the time we got the bed, we hardly had sex any more. It is said that only in our bedrooms do we show our *honne*, our true self. I think our true selves must be very very small, like little children or else, our true selves shrink as we get older in order to fit into our bedrooms. With the bed in there, there was no place in our room for my real self or my husband's. That, maybe, is why our marriage failed.

Have you noticed my feet? I don't think so. If you had

you would not come back to me. Look at them now. See how ugly and twisted they are? My feet are crooked like an old woman's, the knuckle bone beneath my big toe sticks out like an extra thumb, the three last toes are twisted like claws. My feet weren't always like this. Life has made them this way. In the beginning they must have been soft and small and maybe my mother kissed them the way I used to kiss my son Akira's feet when he was a baby. He had the most adorable feet in the world. They were like two tiny cushions; you poked them and immediately the flesh wrapped itself around your finger. Honestly, it felt as if his feet were kissing you. Poor Aki-chan. So delicate and loving. If someone was mean to him he just took the hurt inside himself and hid it there. That is why he had to drop out of school. For the space inside him became full of pain and he could not study any more.

My husband's feet were huge—hard farmers' feet—the kind that planted themselves very deliberately on the ground. They were also surprisingly white. At night, when he would put his feet on my stomach, they would glow like two half moons. Only with his feet touching me could he sleep properly, he would say. When we were still living under the same roof I knew the mark of his feet better than I knew my own hands. Or maybe the mark was actually a hollow carved out from all the nights we slept together in the same bed in the same house. In the beginning his feet filled the hollow inside me, weighing me down so I wouldn't disappear. Later it wasn't enough any more.

Nowadays, when I think of my daughter Haruka's feet, I have to guess what they look like. I cannot remember ever having looked at them closely. Instead, I see my mother's feet which remained small and narrow in spite of the hours she stood on them night after night. They were honourable

Japanese feet. For she sacrificed everything for us, her children. Even her honour.

I like to remember her as she looked the day before my father died. She was wearing a peach-coloured kimono with white clouds and silver cranes flying across the base and the sleeves. Her obi was purple and crimson and her zouri were of brocade, the same fabric as the obi, for the slippers had been made especially for my mother. Her socks were a startling white. In those days few Tokyo streets had hard surfaces. Most streets were a mix of stone paving and mud. How could one walk in Tokyo streets and keep the socks white? As if she had read my mind she said, "A Japanese woman always keeps her socks clean. Otherwise she brings shame to her family." I didn't think it was possible, so I waited for my mother to return and when she finished with the bathroom I rushed in to examine her socks. And there they were, as white as when she had left the house.

The feet are the mirror of the soul. That is why one can never show one's bare feet to the world. We are amazed at how you Westerners wear your shorts and your sandals without socks, showing off your pale white big ugly feet. Even when we wear sandals we always wear stockings. It is a question of politeness, of not imposing oneself upon another. When I was young I had really pretty feet, even smaller and prettier than my mother's. My nails were moon-shaped and clear pink, my soles were nicely arched, my toes were slim. Everything fit well in a neat little package. But because my feet were never seen I had nothing I could be proud of in myself till I bought my first pair of high heels.

High heels are exactly the opposite of the geta. One has only to look at the two together to see just how inferior the geta is. A geta is a block of wood mounted on two smaller blocks placed at right angles under it. On the top is a strap. No matter what, the geta always looks clumsy and is difficult to walk in, so that the one wearing it is forced to shuffle along humbly. High heels are the opposite. The foot is arched, not flat and so the girl looks as if she is walking on air like a goddess or a fairy. The first time I slipped my feet into a pair of proper high heels, they weren't Italian but French, Louis Vuitton. I didn't know much about foreign shoes. But the shop was the same one where I bought my bag. When I slipped my feet into them I felt so strange, so different. As if I belonged in the sky. I felt so good I didn't want to ever take them off again. Seeing the look on my face the salesgirl said helpfully, "Shall I put your old shoes into the bag and would you like to keep wearing these?" My heart was so full of feeling that I could not answer. But she understood anyway and I walked out of the shop a changed person. I could only stare at my shadow in astonishment. Who was that person with such long legs? Suddenly it came to me that I was at last looking the way I was meant to look, that I had at last become who God had meant me to be all along.

The pain came afterwards, when I took off the shoes. My calves began to burn and needles of fire ran up and down my legs. I could not feel my toes and when I tried to move them they wouldn't cooperate. Worst of all, the soles of my feet felt as if I had been walking all night on burning coals. But as I hobbled around my kitchen, preparing the children's evening meal, I felt wonderful—as if I were still in my heels, being devoured by a thousand admiring eyes. So I didn't feel angry with the pain, for it was the other side of my happiness. And, right there inside my small messy home that smelt of fish, I was as happy as I had never been before. That is when I realised that pain can be good. Through it, you can remember and relive an experience more intensely. The pain also took away my guilt. For all afternoon I had been a bad girl, thinking only about myself and spending the money I had intended to keep for others.

The next morning the pain had vanished and I was ready to be bad again.

The first two times the strangers in suits came to see my father, they took off their shoes. I remember them well for one of them took my chin in his hand and, lifting up my face, remarked, "Look, this one will be pretty when she gets older." I was ten then, and I remember feeling both shy and pleased that such a powerful man had noticed me. I didn't have breasts yet, but he must have found something in my face worth noticing. I know now that he only did it to frighten my father into returning the money he owed. The second time they came, my father gave them stolen money, money that he had taken illegally from the company he worked for. The third time the men in suits came, they never took off their shoes. I feel shocked when I think of it. Then I remember how beautiful their shoes were, hand-crafted Italian leather with a strange design in holes on the toe and heel and an "F" emblazoned on the side. I remember how small and naked my father looked lying face down before those shoes, begging for his life, tears streaming down his face. As if he was in ecstasy before the beauty of those shoes. I was the one who had let them in and followed after them into my home. My mother had taken my brother and gone out so I was alone in the house with my father. The big man, the one who had taken my face in his hands, took me outside after they had spoken to my father and bought me an ice cream. When I returned, my father was dead. I never saw it. My mother, though, knew what was going to happen. She told me he was gone when she came to collect me from the neighbours and take us, my brother and I, to our new home.

The Happy Religion

Do you know we have not three but four religions in Japan? We grew up with three: Shintoism, Buddhism, and Christianity. But in the sixties a new religion came to Japan and took many of us away from the older religions. This religion has no name so I have given it one—I call it Happyism. This is the religion that Americans brought us. That is why we didn't kill their soldiers when they came to rule us. Instead, we sent our children to study at American universities. I am the first generation of Japanese to practise Happyism. As you will see, I am in fact somewhat of an expert on it.

Like any other religion, Happyism needed its temples. And in Tokyo we have as many temples to Happyism as we have to Shintoism or Buddhism. The happy temples have different names, Takashimaya, Mitsukoshi, Isetan, Odakyu, Sogo, Lumine, Parco, Seibu. Perhaps you recognize some of the names? Have you been inside a Japanese department store? Only Isetan. That is what I thought. It is where the foreigners go. You should visit Mitsukoshi in Nihonbashi. That is where the really elegant ladies go.

It looks like a European palace with columns and carving and gold plasterwork on the façade. Two stone lions guard the entrance and the doors themselves are inlaid with many precious woods in the Italian style. The windows and light fixtures are European too. And the marble is real Italian. A handsome doorman opens the door and, inside, a pretty woman greets you, "Welcome. Can I be of assistance?" If she recognizes you, she bends even lower and her voice grows even more polite. She will remain bent deferentially till you move inside.

Here, five tiers of gold filigree balconies lead the eye up to a ceiling of translucent glass that gives the entering daylight a milky brightness. Straight ahead are the stairs, a double staircase worthy of the most elegant palace. And just above the stairway, at the first mezzanine, is a giant four-storey-high colourful porcelain Goddess of Good fortune. When I see her I always feel happy. We are here to have fun, she seems to be saying, and to be happy. Happiness is like wine, I think. Good French wine. You drink it and then you want more and more. Then you feel dizzy and if you continue to drink, either you cry or you fall asleep. When you wake up, you are empty and ready to be filled again.

Just as new wine brings an empty glass to life, we come to life inside the *departo*. The air is cool and dry in summer, warm and moist in winter. It is never too dry or too wet. From the air temperature and lighting to the soft voices of the shopgirls and the classical music that is always playing in the background, everything is designed to soothe the spirit and to keep the chaos of the outside world at bay. The money inside my handbag throbs self-importantly. We are ready to begin. But first there is a little preparation. Just as before entering a temple one must wash away the outside world, here we must first change our face. So we pass the Gigantic Happy Goddess and go to the cosmetics tables on the other side where experts wait to give us our new faces.

A face without make-up is like feet without socks. Every day we cover our faces in powder before going out. The face is then neutral—it cannot give away the wearer's secrets. And it cannot disturb others. Eye make-up for a married woman or office lady is always light. It is the cheeks and nose that matter. They must be well covered in a neutral non-shiny powder. And the lips should be painted discreetly.

But here in the *departo* they can change all that. The girls at the cosmetics counter can gently wipe away your imperfect face and replace it with that of a supermodel. They can dress your skin in shimmering colours—base, highlighter, blush and a powder so fine it makes dust look fat. They can make the cracks in the lips disappear and make the lips fuller and brighter. They know how to make the eyes softer, larger, sexy or mysterious. When they are finished with you, your lips look like roses dusted with raindrops. And your beauty rivals that of models on a catwalk. Except that our catwalk is an escalator that leads us up to the women's clothes sections on the second and third floors.

We pay and with our new faces, we take the escalators. What a beautiful thing an escalator is—like walking on the back of a snake. You move but you don't have to move a muscle. You are airborne but you are suspended, your aching feet are soothed, relieved that they have no work to do. So we stand straighter, taller. We lift our chins and look eagerly ahead. What will we find today in the club? How will the things we buy rewrite the story of our lives?

As we move up effortlessly on the very silent and very expensive new escalator, we feel a growing excitement, an eagerness that crowds out all other feelings. We feel empty but happy because we know that the emptiness will soon be filled.

Then comes the special feeling that we have been waiting for, the feeling that brings us back to the *departo* again and again. It starts as a light tickly feeling in the toes, like little bubbles invading every cell in the body. But that is only the beginning. After the happy bubbly feeling dies down, focus and quiet enter the mind as the day's hunt begins.

As in any other game, there are rules in this hunt. The first is to start at the top. This is the first and most important rule, for it teaches you control and discipline. Only when you have mastered these will the gods of desire listen to you. The second rule is simpler. Never buy what is on display. It is what pleases the simplest and least intelligent buyer. It is also what is least expensive to make but costs the most. Third, avoid shopgirls. Don't make eye contact. They are masters of deceit and creators of obstacles. They will confuse you with their words and smiles, their insincere flattery. And fourth, know what it is you are looking for before you enter the golden doors. This is the hardest rule to follow, for the happy feeling pushes every other thought aside.

Those who survive in my club are like samurai. They pursue their goals in a highly disciplined way, following the rules. If you write these rules into your body you too can become a warrior. If you do not, your cupboards will fill with useless things even as your pocket empties. But as in love, when you finally find that one magic thing, the one piece of clothing or accessory that is meant for you, your heart fills with gratitude. Yes, gratitude, for you feel touched by the gods. You were chosen. You are the winner. You rush past all the other focused, intelligent, beautiful women doing exactly what you are doing and you quickly grab the object of your desire and look for the nearest changing room. If you are an experienced member like me, you don't need to search, you know where they are. The architecture of the *departo* is imprinted on your brain.

And now we come to the heart of my club. The place we women like best—the changing room. Entering a changing room is like being alone with your loved one for the first time. Now is the moment when you can hold your prize in your hands and taste the pleasure of ownership. Separated from prying eyes, you can touch your prize, kiss it and finally, enter it. Inside the changing room, you savour your privacy. Here you take possession for the first time.

Once I am satisfied, I return with my prize to the sales counter. Do you know why no club member ever steals? Because then they would never be able to re-enter the club and there can be no punishment worse than that. The bubbles inside my body begin to diminish, but grow again as I think of all that I will have to buy to provide my purchase with the right frame for its beauty. A new dress is only a beginning and I must plan the rest, right down to the colour and design of the stockings. And so the money you give me in exchange for my body is well spent.

And I am happy. And the happy feeling will last till I return to my room. Thanks to Americans we learnt about Happyism. And now we want the whole world to be happy and to buy, buy and buy like we do. Then there will be world peace.

Part Two

Tomoko

You look surprised. I like you when you look surprised. Perhaps that is why I am telling you my secret thoughts. When I first began to tell you these things I felt guilty. Now I know that there is no need. One feels guilty when one does something that is not natural. What I am doing is not only natural but obvious. A secret envy binds the members of my club together. It is this envy that drives us to buy and buy, and the bond it creates is more powerful than love. But women's envy is special. There are no hierarchies amongst women, so all women are free to envy all other women. For we all know that what we do does not matter. We are interchangeable. A woman's duties and her place in the world are decided by men. It doesn't matter whether a woman works in an office or at home, the outcome is the same. That is why we housewives hate the office ladies and the office ladies hate us. For no matter how different we try to make ourselves, we know that underneath we are all the same.

Amongst us housewives, it is even worse. It doesn't matter which club we belong to, whether it is the tennis club or the shoppers club or the health club or the joggers club or the ikebana club or the charity club, not only are our houses the same, our routines, our lives are the same. Do you know that on Mondays if you don't go early to the supermarket you cannot find any marinated cod-fish? And on Tuesdays, it is the beef that is in short supply. On Thursdays it is red snapper and prawn. And on Friday, everything is difficult to find and so we all buy eggs. Can you believe it? We are so alike that even the food we feed our families is the same. So why should our children not also be exactly the same?

This is our greatest fear.

The only way to rise above our sameness is to turn our children into superheroes. They must defeat all the others and get the best results and the most prizes. Then and only then can we be sure that we have succeeded. But to make children who are superheroes, we must first become superheroes ourselves. So we housewives work hard, and we make our children work even harder. We don't complain, just focus on the objective till we obtain it. Or fall down dead, which we rarely do, unlike the men.

How is that possible? Is this woman mad? I can read your face, you know. I am a superwoman. I know what that look means.

The road to superwoman status is veiled in mystery and will always be so. But I will tell you where it lies. To be a superwoman you need to create a secret garden inside yourself, and in that garden you throw all your filth—everything you cannot say or feel—your tiredness, your anger, your hatred of your family and your responsibilities, the never-changing routine. In the endless silence of the night you watch your evil garden grow. In the day, you stamp it down and you are a superwoman.

But sometimes our garden grows too fast and we cannot see the sky any more. Then we take out the buried half-dead girl inside us. Only she has the strength to stamp out the weeds in our gardens. We put on our pretty clothes and feel pretty and girlie. Or we go to the gym or the temple or whatever other club takes us in and makes us feel special.

That is why our choice of club is so important to us. The club is where we go to find ourselves. The moment we enter our club we feel different. A Buddha-like peace enters our soul. Whether the club is dark and lined in wood and leather or has plastic tiles and neon lights and pop music, the effect upon our soul is the same. We have come home, so we feel happy.

But finding the right club is very difficult. Eventually I suppose I would have joined some boring club like the fitness club or the local ikebana circle. But I was saved from that horrible fate by Tomoko.

I was twenty-seven when I met Tomoko again. The funny thing is, it was she who recognized me first. I didn't recognize her even when she called my name. This is because I was in the middle of one of my *makkura* moments...

Makkura, as you must know, means pure blackness in Japanese. But for me, *makkura* is more than that. It is a place beyond thought, beyond action, where nothing happens, nothing could be done, no decisions taken. It is a place without sound, colour, light. Many women have felt it but they won't talk about it. Instead, some begin to drink, others find god, still others retreat into silence. Some stay there for the rest of their lives. We never speak of it to each other. Like everything we do, we do it in secret.

The *makkura* came into my life when I became pregnant with Haruka. It would descend upon me suddenly, deep and endless, darker than the bottom of the sea on a moonless night, wrapping itself around my mind so completely that I would just sit inside my house, the windows and curtains closed, lights off, and lose all track of time. Sometimes I would forget to collect Akira from primary school and the teacher would call me at home. Then, with great difficulty I would rouse myself and find the energy to get dressed and go get my son.

Sometimes the *makkura* made me late and the other mothers would smile when they saw my messy hair and hastily put on clothes. But nobody offered to help. As in every other thing in a Japanese woman's life, I had to face the *makkura* alone.

On the day I met Tomoko there was no reason at all for the black cloud to have come. It was my birthday. As a surprise present, my husband had arranged for his aunt Asako to collect Akira from school and bring him home and stay with him while he took me to an expensive French restaurant for dinner. Ryu told me this after he woke me up early in the morning. I was still struggling with my surprise as he did what he always did with my breasts, entered me quickly, and finished. So though I could not have an orgasm I was happy and my heart was singing as I dropped Akira at primary school. "What a kind and generous husband I have! How thoughtful he is!" I thought, as I cleaned the house vigorously and cooked the evening meal for Asako-san.

By eleven I was ready. The day stretched before me in a rosy haze. In the shower I made up a riddle: what is the colour of free time once one is married? Pink, of course. I giggled, and then I was laughing so hard I was practically screaming. But luckily the shower blocked out the sound and failed to alert the neighbours. As I walked to the station I tried to plan my day. I would go shopping first and then maybe eat a late lunch after which I would go to a beauty parlour and sleep while they fussed over my nails and my hair. But if the shopping took too long, I would grab an onigiri on the way to the hairdresser. Either way, it was going to be a beautiful day.

I got out of the line at Ginza station, right on the big crossing. It was a beautiful autumn day. The sky was a deep clear blue and the sunshine felt light and welcoming. The streets were full of smart well-dressed people hurrying importantly to their lunches. Normally the sight of so many elegant people would have filled me with excitement. But instead, the happy feeling I'd had inside me all morning, just wasn't there any more.

I stopped suddenly, so suddenly that the man behind bumped into me. I turned to excuse myself but he wouldn't meet my eyes. Then the *makkura* was upon me and it was as though I couldn't see any more, or think or even remember who I was or why I was there.

I have no idea how long I was standing in front of Matsuya department store when I felt a hand on my shoulder. I turned around angrily and saw a tall, beautiful office lady dressed in a rich murasaki, purple, Chanel suit with a forest-green Hermes Kelly bag on her arm. I was about to excuse myself and move out of her way when the stranger's fingers tightened and she said my name. Yes, my name. Not my married name, which is how most people addressed me—but the name my parents gave me when I was born. "Kayo-chan," the woman said, "Don't you know your old school friend Tomoko any more?"

Kayo is not a pretty name so I rarely tell it to people. I was so surprised to hear it in a stranger's mouth that my own mouth must have fallen open in surprise. Suddenly Tomoko laughed, revealing perfect white teeth but with a little gap in the middle of the two upper front ones, and at last I recognized her. I don't remember what I said then or maybe I said nothing at all and she grew impatient, but the next thing I remember was her grabbing my arm and guiding me through the crowd of midday shoppers streaming out of the gates of Matsuya and down a quiet side street.

I was wearing trousers that day that were held up by an elastic band—cheap grandmother pants that are sold at suburban shopping malls for a thousand yen. I had never even crossed glances with an office lady let alone talked to one. And now I was walking beside the most beautiful office lady in all of Ginza, feeling once more the electric charge of aroused men's eyes all around me. I wondered what they thought of me in my ugly clothes and fell back a little out of embarrassment. But as we continued down the street I realised that I needn't have bothered, for as always, Tomoko's beauty cast a deep shadow. I walked invisibly at her side, wondering what the clothes she wore had cost her and what kind of work she did to be able to afford them. From there, I began to wonder about her life: Had she married a millionaire, someone she'd met at college or at work, or was she working for a company? Like a heavy curtain being pulled back, the *makkura* retreated.

Tomoko brought me to Café Renoir, an old-fashioned Ginza coffee house which only served coffee and sponge cakes that oozed fresh cream. I was a bit surprised by her choice as it was lunchtime, but then I realised that since it was twelve-thirty most of the seats at the other restaurants would have been taken already and the restaurants themselves would have been too noisy for us to talk. I stared at her shoes as we walked up the steep wooden stairs. They were of crocodile skin. Prada.

Only when we were seated at a quiet table at the end of the restaurant did I dare look into her face, to find her looking into mine. We were both quiet as we stared openly at each other, trying to pinpoint the changes that time had wrought.

It took me a minute to see the change. Tomoko had always been beautiful but now there was something more: she looked expensive. Like a piece of antique jewellery or a Patek Philippe watch. And that is what made her even more desirable to men. I thought of how they had looked at her on the street, wanting her but knowing they couldn't afford her. How did she do it? It wasn't just the clothes. Other women in Ginza also wore the same things. I looked carefully at her again. Her dyed brown hair was fashionably cut and permed to frame her beautiful face. Her make-up was discreet and well matched. Her skin glowed and her full lips shone as if they had only just been buffed and polished. Her eyes looked larger than they had in the past and their almond-shaped eyelids bore the faintest shimmer of copper eyeshadow. Then my eyes widened as my brain registered what had been done. Her eyelids had been "fixed", a crease inserted in order to make her eyes look larger and more Western.

Tomoko was the first to break the silence. "How wise you were to get married early," she said, a tinge of regret in her voice. "How is married life?"

I could not think. It was like a dream come true when I had long ago stopped believing in dreams. The world grew hazy as the *makkura* tried to get hold of me again. Weakly I noticed Tomoko was speaking again.

"I can't tell you how happy I am to have found you," Tomoko said. "How is Ryu-chan? Is he a good husband to you? Are you happy? Please tell me."

I pressed a hand weakly to my temple, trying to jog free a word or two. How could I speak of my boring life when I was burning with curiosity about hers?

Tomoko's beautiful face clouded with concern. "Oh, how selfish of me. Are you okay? You looked so tired when I tapped your shoulder and you turned to me. Do you know I followed you from the station? I was in the same train. At first I wasn't sure it was you. You looked so grown-up and patient, a real wife and mother. Then you scratched the side of your nose and wrinkled it in a typical Kayo way and I knew it had to be you. I was so happy. I wanted to hug you right there, but I was afraid. What if you didn't remember me? Then I felt bad, bad that I had let you go out of my life and so I thought I had better walk away. But I couldn't and so I followed you." The words spilled out of her so fast I could barely keep them apart. Where did all that energy come from? I wondered. Is that why she was, as one would say, "on the thin side of fashionable"?

A middle-aged waitress in an Austrian milkmaid dress came to take our order. Tomoko ordered for me, taking charge just as she had when we were in school. She ordered the chocolate cake. I opened my mouth to tell her that as I was pregnant, I had to be very careful, but since she was deep in conversation with the waitress I dared not interrupt. After the waitress left, she looked at me apologetically. "The chocolate cake here is the best in Tokyo. I know your doctor must have told you not to eat chocolate but sometimes you have to be bad."

I laughed and the last vestiges of *makkura* vanished. I said the first thing that came into my head. "You've become even more beautiful than you were in school, Tomo-chan."

She had the grace to look a little embarrassed. "It's just the clothes that have changed," she said with a shrug. "Those school uniforms were terrible. But you've changed too. More than I have. Just look at you, you've lost so much weight."

"I haven't," I muttered, feeling proud that she'd noticed all the same. "I am fat and pregnant."

And we were back to our old way of talking to each other, being nice, kind, and supporting each other. For in the world of women, kindness can only exist between unequals.

"No, that is not true," Tomoko insisted. "Your breasts are still big, but the rest of you has become so small. I can hardly see the baby. Is this your first one?"

"No, my second," I replied, feeling even better.

She brightened, "Boy or girl? And how old?"

"Seven years. A boy," I replied.

"Oh how lucky. I want to meet him. Where is he now?"

Tomoko asked eagerly.

"At school. My husband's aunt, Asako-san, is picking him up later and staying with him for the night." I couldn't help boasting a little. "It's my birthday you see, Ryu arranged it."

Tomoko's well-shaped eyebrows went up in surprise. "Ryu? How thoughtful of him."

"Ryu wanted me to go shopping and then meet him after work for dinner," I explained.

"How romantic! After nearly ten years of marriage! I can hardly believe it." Tomoko looked at the floor beside me, and seeing my lack of shopping bags rushed on, "I'm sorry, I've taken you away from your shopping, haven't I? And it is already nearly 1 p.m. When is your hairdresser's appointment? How much time do you have? I am so sorry. How inconsiderate of me! Let's pay here, and then let me take you shopping. I want to get you a present also. I forgot it was your birthday."

"But... but, what about your office?" I stammered. "Don't you have to go back soon?"

But Tomoko wasn't at all concerned. "Oh don't worry about that. I'll tell them I was with a client."

"What... what kind of work do you do?" I asked curiously, sensing something new had just entered Tomoko, something that made her seem suddenly more alive, and more beautiful than she had been a few moments earlier.

"Many things," she said evasively. "I'm a shopping consultant."

"I see." I was quiet, trying to imagine what her job involved. "Do you advise department stores on what to buy for their clients?" I asked.

"I tell very rich people, film stars and baseball player's wives, what to buy," she snapped. Looking pointedly at her watch, she added, "Let's go, I have only one hour." Tomoko paid for us and we walked out into the autumn sunlight, all brilliance and little warmth. Tomoko steered me once more towards Matsuya Department store. On the way she suddenly became very business-like and asked me all kinds of questions about my clothes size and bra size, my weight, height and favourite colours.

Lastly she asked, "And have you got a certain 'mood' or 'look' in mind for this evening?"

"Mood?' I stammered. "What do you mean?"

"A mood—you know, vamp kitten, sulky chic, sexy, innocent, girly, Western. There are so many, what kind of evening do you have in mind?"

I looked at Tomoko in amazement. It had never occurred to me that I could influence the evening by what I would wear. "There is no plan really," I said. "Just that Ryu is taking me to dinner and so I was going to buy a new dress."

Tomoko looked at me pityingly. Just as when I'd told her I was going to marry Ryu. That skinny quiet guy, her eyes had said. "Just a dress? Have you got shoes and a bag with which you want to match the dress?" she asked.

"No, I just want something nice for the French restaurant, a little formal but pretty. Maybe in black. But if I can't find a nice dress I am quite happy with a shirt. I don't mind." I smiled nervously, knowing that I didn't understand at all what Tomoko wanted. We belonged quite clearly in two different Japans. The one she lived in clearly didn't think twice about spending *jyuman en* (100,000 yen) on a dress. Whereas I, at that stage, felt bad about spending more than 30,000 on any piece of clothing.

As if she'd read my thoughts, Tomoko said coldly, "If 'new' is all you want, you will be wasting your money for sure." She looked me over critically, and I knew she was calculating the cost of what I had on. But then her face brightened. "Lucky for you I found you," she said, grabbing my arm. "Come along, we are going to give Ryu a surprise."

Inside the department store, Tomoko fired even more questions at me. "Your hair," she said, "why have you not dyed it? It is so old-fashioned. And besides, black hair makes you look old."

I touched my hair self-consciously. "I haven't had time. Because of my child," I said stiffly.

Tomoko laughed. "Look at those women there," she said, pointing to a group of beautiful women in dark dresses and pearls. "They are mothers too."

I looked in the direction of her pointing finger and saw that the women indeed all had brown hair.

"How do you know that they are mothers?" I asked curiously.

"The same way you knew I was an office lady," she replied.

Then, looking me over critically, she said, "You know what you really need? A haircut. And you must change the colour of your hair. Then no matter what you wear you will look elegant. The secret of looking elegant, I tell you, is in the hair." While she said the last bit she was busily searching for something in her bag. "Here," she said triumphantly, "I knew I had one. The best-kept secret in Tokyo. My hairdresser Rockie. After this I will take you to him and get you fixed— he is very busy but will do it for me." I wanted to ask how much it would cost but while I hesitated over the words she had turned and was walking quickly to the escalators. As usual, all I could do was follow.

While we went up she asked, "Do you have any brands you prefer? What brands do you buy normally?"

I didn't dare tell her that I didn't know many brands. "Louis Vuitton," I said promptly.

Tomoko looked a little scornful. "You should try the Italian brands. They are better, both for clothes and for shoes. What colour are they, your shoes?"

"Brown leather," I replied.

"That's easy to match." She sounded relieved. I clutched my handbag tightly to my side, imagining the money that would soon be flying out of it. Tomoko must have noticed, for she smiled reassuringly. "This is my birthday present to you. To make up for all the birthdays I missed, not to mention your marriage."

"You missed nothing," I said uneasily.

We got off on the second floor, where all the expensive clothes by Western brands were displayed. I hung back, too ashamed of myself to follow. How could someone dressed the way I was dare to get off the escalator here, I thought. This floor was for the Tomokos of the world. I turned to go. But then it struck me that if I left now I would never see Tomoko again, so I hesitated. Sensing the lack of footsteps behind her, Tomoko stopped and turned. "Come on," she said impatiently from the far end of the corridor, "don't get distracted so easily, it is fatal."

And so, instead of making my escape as I had wanted to, I let Tomoko take over.

It is said that when there is no-one else to fall in love with, one falls in love with oneself. But you cannot fall in love with yourself if there is nothing beautiful to fall in love with. Tomoko showed me what to love in myself. When I put on the clothes she chose for me, I saw someone else—a person I could love.

We walked in and out of one expensive store after another. Tomoko was at her best—haughty, arrogant, beautiful. Every step we took together I fell more and more under her spell. I loved the way the shopgirls danced around her, bringing dress after dress, ensemble after ensemble. In the end, Tomoko made me buy a simple dress in a dull gold, the colour of fallen leaves. I looked at the price tag and got a shock: 310,000 yen! Up until then I had never heard of a Valentino and the clothes seemed rather ridiculous to me. I was already shaking my head and giving it back to the salesgirl when Tomoko interceded, "No, please. I insist. Just try it on. It will suit you." So I went into the changing area and I put on the gold dress.

When I looked at myself, I no longer needed to be convinced. The dress showed off my breasts and its skilful folds hid my growing stomach. The simple fabric made me seem taller than I was, and its rich colour added a glow to my pale skin. I stared at my bare shoulders and knew that all the men in the restaurant would be looking at me that night.

When I shyly opened the curtain and walked out, even the salesgirl seemed impressed.

As for me, I looked at myself in the mirror and then looked away, afraid that if I looked too hard the old me would resurface. "Good, we'll take this one," Tomoko announced, coming and standing behind me. "See, I told you it would suit you." I looked at our two reflections side by side and to my surprise I realised that we didn't look so different any more. The dress had changed that. Then, as if I was waking reluctantly from a beautiful dream, I remembered the price.

"I cannot take it, it is too expensive," I muttered. It was the last time I ever used those words.

"Don't be silly," Tomoko said. "You must take it. Clothes are the only real power we women have in this world." She bent towards me and lowered her voice, "And they are the best medicine."

"Wh... what do you mean?" I asked, wondering if Tomoko knew about *makkura*.

I understood exactly what Tomoko meant. In that dress the *makkura* could not touch me. "It's just beautiful, thank you," I said when the salesgirl handed me the bag with the dress.

The salesgirl bowed and as we were leaving she said impulsively, "You are lucky to have a wonderful friend."

I was surprised. "I know," I said, glancing at Tomoko. "Thank you."

On the escalator, a new and disturbing thought filled my mind. I worried that my husband would notice that it was an expensive dress of a kind I had never ever bought before and ask me what it cost. How could I explain that it was a gift from an old school friend? It sounded false even to my ears.

Right there and then, I decided I would lie. I would not abandon my new clothes. I knew Ryu. I knew what he would believe. I could easily make up a story that would satisfy him. Already I felt protective towards my new clothes as if they were my babies. When we got to the first floor, Tomoko turned and looked at me critically. "I think you need something for your neck," she announced.

I held my Louis Vuitton bag protectively in front of my chest. "M... my neck? I don't understand."

But Tomoko wasn't looking at me any more, she was struggling with the clasp of her own necklace. When at last it dangled between us, the diamonds flashing blue fire in the light, I gasped, "I cannot take that."

"It's not a gift. Just a loan. You can give it back to me when we meet next," she answered. "Beauty is not enough, you know. To make a man want her, a woman must look expensive."

Immediately I understood what she meant. "How do you know so much about men?" I asked boldly.

Tomoko laughed. But it wasn't a nice sound. "We will keep that story for another day," she said firmly.

"But your husband... I mean your fiancé, won't he notice...?" I asked. I hoped she hadn't noticed that my eyes had gone briefly to her ringless hand.

Her mouth turned down at the edges as she replied somewhat bitterly, "He won't notice."

I suppose my own mouth must have fallen open for she gave a twisted smile and ice touched her face.

"Yes, really," she said.

"But... but," I stammered, "you're so beautiful."

She smiled in acknowledgement. "I'm free, as I always wanted to be," she said, "and I don't belong to any man.'"

And with that, Tomoko killed me.

For until I met Tomoko again I had thought I was free, or at least had a life that was of my own choosing. But meeting Tomoko again made me realise that I was in fact a prisoner. And that the walls of my prison were not made of stone and cement but of hours and minutes. And because time is invisible, my prison was impossible to destroy. So a terrible desire was born in me. I had to escape my prison.

From that day on I stopped being myself, consumed by one sole desire—to learn everything I could about Tomoko. I wanted to know every tiny detail of her life, whether she ate a Western or Japanese breakfast, where she sat in her office, what she did before she went to work, what make-up she used, who she worked with, how she decorated her house and most importantly, who she slept with. Did she have many lovers, or just one? Did she make them pay for her or did she give herself for free?

I wanted to taste every last drop of her life—so I could take her place. I could think of nothing else.

The enormity of the task I had set myself should have plunged me into despair. But it didn't. For I had never forgotten who I had seen hiding in my shadow on that baseball field by Yotsuya station all those years ago.

Beautiful Things – 1

The problem with beautiful things is that when you have one, you want two and when you have two, you want three. For the eye's hunger has no limit. Unlike the mouth which has a bag—the stomach—attached to it, the eye is simply an opening. Behind it is the bottomless cupboard of the mind.

The American soldiers, when they came to Japan after WWII, gave their "girls" sheer nylon stockings as presents. Till then, ordinary Japanese women did not wear Western clothes except if they worked in a Western-style office or if they came from a very westernized Christian high-class family. But by the time the Americans left, city women from all social classes were wearing Western clothes. Department stores like Mitsukoshi and Isetan which had begun as kimono shops were selling eighty per cent Western clothes. Do you know why this is so? Because stockings fulfilled a deep need in us. They made us feel cared for and beautiful.

Stockings killed the kimono and I am glad they did. I think stockings were what brought many Japanese women into my club, maybe even what created the club. But they didn't bring me into the club, Tomoko brought me in. She showed me that clothes were magic, that life could become exciting just by wearing the right clothes. She also taught me that wearing beautiful clothes made one special, just as wearing boring clothes made one boring. "Just burn all your clothes," she would tell me, "and let me choose new ones for you." And such was her power that when I was with her I felt sure that if I were to go home and do just that, my life would change.

Unlike when we were girls, now every time we met, we went shopping. I think Tomoko must have been doing this for some time, for all the shopgirls on Aoyama Dori knew her. Sometimes she'd call late at night, around midnight, when Ryu and I were already asleep. But she never apologised. "What are you doing tomorrow?" she'd say in her sexiest voice. "You want to come to Tokyo and have fun?" Of course I wanted to. I was dying to have fun. For, my life with Ryu was the opposite of fun.

We would meet around noon. Tomoko would pick me up at the mouth of the metro station, usually Ebisu or Omotesando, looking incredibly beautiful and glamorous. Then we would go to a fashionable restaurant of Tomoko's choice and have lunch. Tomoko would chatter gaily about the latest fashions, scandals and people. The way she talked, it seemed she knew everyone the magazines were talking about. Since she was so beautiful and so tall and well-dressed, every head would turn when we entered. Tomoko pretended not to notice but I knew she liked the attention. All through lunch she would sparkle, telling me one story after the other about the parties she went to, art gallery openings, store openings, fashion parties and their after parties. She described the women she met (but never the men) and what they wore and the silly things they said. I would listen politely, laugh at the right moments, but my heart would burn with envy. And so I was always hungry for more details about her life, and the men she met and slept with, not just the lives of people I had never heard of.

Afterwards we would go shopping and once again Tomoko would be transformed. The languid waiting feeling that often clung to her and made her seem like an Edo bijinga heroine would completely disappear and she would drag me from shop to shop like a tigress on a hunt.

And what an expert hunter she was! Where I hung back bewildered by the sheer number and variety of clothes on sale, she would go through the shop and be inside the trial room within a matter of minutes, astounding the salesgirl with the elegance of her combinations.

"Wonderful! Are you a model?" they would ask her. And Tomoko would smile as she shook her head. "Just an office lady," she'd reply. "Are you buying this for a special date? He will certainly ask you to marry him if you wear that," they'd say when she bought the sexiest dress in the shop. And Tomoko would laugh with them, looking even more beautiful than before. I wished I could ask her who he was, and what he looked like. But I didn't dare, knowing instinctively that Tomoko's face would close and she would shut me out of her world. As she tried on pair after pair of elegant high heels, I would try to imagine him. Certainly he was rich, for Tomoko spent money like water, half a million yen on a Valentino outfit, sometimes even more. And certainly young and handsome—for a girl as beautiful as Tomoko, who could have any man she wanted, would surely choose only the best.

But shopping did something else to Tomoko and it was this that truly made me want to be like her. It seemed to fill her soul. As we walked from shop to shop, her face would glow with an inner light. She seemed terribly sexy then, and strong, like a lioness who'd just eaten, or a woman who'd had amazing sex. Women would stare at her, unable to tear their eyes away. She was like an invitation to pleasure. Cars would stop and men would roll down their windows and call to her. I felt proud to be beside her then, prouder even than I had felt when we were in school.

When at last she'd finished for the day, we would go with our shopping bags to a dimly lit café on the first floor of a building in Aoyama. There the waiters would place special baskets beside our chairs for us to put our purchases in and, as we waited for our coffees and cream cakes and the sky gradually lost its brightness, the light inside her would gradually dim. Emptiness would creep into her face as she lit cigarette after cigarette, looking towards the windows of the coffee shop as if she were expecting someone.

I would try to break the silence by asking Tomoko questions about herself. But she would never give me a direct answer. But when I would ask her if she was all right, she'd immediately shake her head and laugh and fire questions at me and talk a lot for about five minutes. Then she would lapse into silence again and her eyes would dodge from window to restaurant entrance to window again. We'd sit like that, not saying much, till night fell and I had to return home.

Maybe Tomoko sensed there was something unnatural about my curiosity. Cleverly she kept her personal life behind a curtain, never inviting me to visit her home or introducing me to her friends. One time, when we were in Nihonbashi Mitsukoshi, a Japanese man who was accompanying a very chic foreign woman with short blonde hair, waved at us. But Tomoko pretended not to have seen her and taking my arm firmly led me out of the department store. And so each time I would take the train home from Shibuya after spending the day with Tomoko I was frustrated. But by the time I got home, I would be looking forward again to the next time I'd see her. For there would be a next time, that I was certain of. And eventually Tomoko would have to confide in me: for by then, without her saying it, I knew she had no friends.

In the meantime I was happy to wait.

Those months before my daughter Haruka's birth were the happiest ones of my life. Tomoko was a great teacher. I learnt to fend off pushy salesgirls with a glance. I learnt to choose with care. When I found something that was right for me and held it against myself I almost believed I had begun to look just a little like her and when Tomoko nodded and said yes, that is just what she would wear, I immediately took out my credit card or my husband's, not even looking at the price. My mother's money felt like a red carpet stretching eternally in front of me. I bought and bought. Even if they were all clothes I couldn't wear. And I was happy. The *makkura* that had troubled me so much earlier had completely disappeared and never came back. For Tomoko had made me see that magic existed even in the dull adult world.

When Haruka was born, Tomoko came to visit me at the hospital. I was surprised to see her there. She looked out of place, like a sailor on shore leave. Ryu was even more surprised than I was. But once he'd overcome the shock he looked happy. Tomoko on the other hand looked ill at ease and after looking quickly at the baby and inquiring politely about its birth, she left. She had of course bought a very expensive present for me and Haruka—an adjustable sling made of organic African cotton which all the Hollywood star mothers used to carry their babies around. After she left, Ryu asked me all sorts of questions about her. But by the end of our conversation it was clear that he knew more about the intervening years of her life than I did. He knew that she had graduated with a degree in business management from Tokyo University and that she had joined a prestigious firm of accountants. Then after six years she had left. No-one knew why. But after that even Ryu's best friend, Yasuo, who had been dating Tomoko when we were in high school and had remained friends with her after they broke up, had lost touch with her. I told him what Tomoko had told me, that she was working as a consultant to a big American millionaire. But when he asked me the name I couldn't remember. I wasn't sure if she'd ever mentioned his name.

I was surprised to see Ryu look so animated. That is why I remember that day. And also because it was the only time, outside of shopping time, that I felt truly happy: Ryu, Tomoko and I together in the same room making me feel like a girl again. After she left, Ryu said wistfully, "Maybe now that you two have found each other she will visit our house sometimes."

"Of course she will," I agreed. But in my heart I knew she wouldn't come.

At first, secretly, I was glad. For when we were on the streets of Tokyo we were equals but inside my drab little house with its cardboard walls and tiled exterior our differences would rise up like a wall and separate us forever. I figured she would call me eventually. In the meantime I was quite happy to wait.

But after Haruka began to sleep regularly and I had become used to the extra work, my mind grew restless. I would open my cupboard and see all the beautiful things we had bought together, Tomoko and I, and feel sad. Though I was slim once again and could have worn any of them, without Tomoko there was no reason to wear them and no place to go. My expensive clothes stared at me reproachfully. I had betrayed them.

A year passed. Though I tried to call her many times, Tomoko never answered the phone, and never returned my calls either. So I decided I would go and look for her. Haruka was one and I had found a crèche for her. I was slimmer even than I had been before and was dying to go shopping again.

It was 1998, the "bubble" economy had ended but we didn't feel it. Most salaried men still had mistresses. They went to geisha houses and hostess bars every evening. They bought Hermes bags for their wives and Louis Vuitton for their girlfriends. The wives shopped. The office ladies shopped. The mistresses shopped. Everyone shopped. Even Ryu, normally so careful with his money, sold our house and took out a fresh loan from his bank for a bigger, Western-style house in Den-en-Chofu. He gave me another credit card and told me to buy whatever I wanted for the new house. In the glorious enchantment of shopping for our new house I forgot about my unanswered calls to Tomoko. I left her messages on her phone so she knew what I was doing, what I was buying. I told her about the house. But still she didn't return my calls. Then one day Ryu came home and announced that I would have to take English classes.

"Why?" I cried. "Don't you think I have enough to do looking after this big house?"

"Yes, yes I know you do," Ryu rushed to agree with me, "but I am going to change jobs. I am joining an American bank."

"What? When did you decide this? Why didn't you consult me?" I screamed.

Ryu's face grew stiff. "I didn't know for sure till yesterday. We signed the contract last night."

"So that's why you came home at five in the morning!" I accused. "You were celebrating."

Ryu nodded shamefacedly. "American companies are different. Wives are part of the company too. You will have to help me entertain business guests. That is why I want you to learn English."

I said nothing. I had been terrible in English in school. If it hadn't been for Tomoko's skilful preparation I would never have passed the tests. The idea of going back to school terrified me.

"Don't worry. You will be fine. *Gambatte*. I know how smart you are."

I shook my head, a little numb. "But this house... the kids. How will I find the time to study?" I said weakly.

Ryu frowned. "Do it for me, please. I start the new job in three months. At double my old salary." He leaned over the table and to my surprise kissed me on the lips. "In twenty years this house will be ours."

Maybe you have guessed it.

Tomoko cannot give me an answer because Tomoko is dead. She threw herself in front of a train, yes, a boring suburban train just like the one I take from my home in Chofu to Tokyo every day. Only Tomoko chose a very public time to do it, seven-thirty in the morning, when the trains are full of salaried men and women going to work. As I wait for the train to come, I think of her standing there, waiting for the train to arrive. What was she thinking in those last minutes? Did she think of her parents, of her lover, of me maybe? Or did she think of herself? She must have looked beautiful even then, as she waited for the train to come. First there would have been the polite announcement of the arrival of the train in the stationmaster's impersonal electronic voice. Tomoko's body would have tensed. Was she happy then? Did her body give a slight jerk and betray her or did she control herself so beautifully that no-one could tell? It must have been cold on the platform in mid-March. (The cherry blossom buds had appeared but hadn't yet bloomed. Everyone was waiting for them. Cherry blossom time is the happiest time in Japan. You must come to Tokyo then.) Within a minute

72

of the announcement, Tomoko would have heard the train, and then she would have felt the vibration. Her head would have come up. She would have seen the light go from red to green and then she'd have seen the train itself, a giant silver snake emerging magically out of the early-morning mist. Did she look up at the sky as she fell? Did she see the unopened buds of the sakura and imagine that like them she too would soon begin a new clean life? Or did the sight of them fill her with sadness, knowing that she would not be there to see them open? Whenever I think these thoughts I feel happy. I feel grateful that I am alive and that I am going to get onto the train and go to Tokyo and hunt for beautiful things to wear. When I see the sakura branches swelling with life I am filled with the urge to go shopping.

But what was Tomoko doing on a suburban railway line at seven-thirty in the morning at the start of the rush hour? I think she must have become tired of waiting. Perhaps her lover had promised to come and see her and hadn't shown up? Perhaps he'd told her that he would stay the night so she'd gone shopping, bought a new dress, new underwear, and new perfume. She would have bought the best pre-prepared meal she could find in her local supermarket or ordered a nine-course kaiseki meal from a nearby restaurant. Then she would have sat down to wait. At ten maybe she called him and he didn't answer. She tried five, ten times in the next hour. Then it was time for the last metro. So she got her coat and without bothering to fix her make-up, which must have been all gone, for, without doubt she'd have been crying, she went out, took a taxi to Shibuya and then got on his suburban train line. She got off at his stop and then walked to his house. Maybe the curtains were open. Maybe she watched him play with his children and put them to bed. Maybe she watched him eat food prepared by his wife and watch television together. And when the two of them went up the stairs and the lights were finally turned off in the little house in the suburbs, maybe she went to a bar, the only place still open at that time of night, and sat there drinking till it closed. In the early morning she must have gone to the toilet, fixed her face, and maybe then went to the Jonathan's next door for breakfast. Afterwards she would have walked over to the station, bought her last metro ticket. Maybe she killed herself because she realised that the man she had been waiting for was worthless.

Beautiful Things – 2

I found out about Tomoko's death six months after she was gone. I got tired of waiting for Tomoko to return my calls and decided to visit her. I still had the *meishi* she had given me when we first met. I had only ever used the mobile number on it but there were a series of other numbers and an address as well. So one day, after dropping my son at school and leaving Haruka in the care of the local obaa-chan, I took the Tokyu-Toyoko line to Shibuya and, with a map in hand, I went looking for Tomoko's office.

But when I arrived at the right address I couldn't believe my eyes. It wasn't some grey, anonymous office building as I had imagined but one of those new private condominium apartment buildings built for *gaikokujin*, foreigners. The building was all glass and fifteen floors high. The entrance itself stuck out into the street, a simple glass cube, everything visible inside, with a wall of Italian marble at the far end in front of which was a counter as in a hotel with a uniformed person behind it. I was staring helplessly at the buttons on the console beside the automatic door, wondering which ones to press for Tomoko's office, when the doors opened and someone walked out. I didn't hesitate, I walked straight in. Viewed from the inside the lobby was even more luxurious. Through the glass windows on the right I saw a mini zen garden with white stones, a sakura tree and a little stream running through it.

In front of the windows were two benches of white leather facing the garden. I must admit I was impressed and not a little intimidated. Then the black-suited man came up to me and asked if he could assist me—just as they would in a hotel. I took out the card from my pocket, and showed it to him. "I am looking for Yamada Holdings Pvt. Ltd," I said.

The man took the rather beaten-up card with great respect and stared at it silently. "Who do you want to meet?" he asked cautiously. "Do you have an appointment?"

"I've come to meet her, Tomoko Ohara. She's my friend," I said impatiently, "Only she forgot to tell me there was a code." The concierge had beautiful manners. He didn't look up immediately. "She was your friend? I'm so sorry."

At first the use of the past tense didn't register. But when he looked me full in the face, I understood. The world began to spin, the white leather bench, the stones in the zen garden, the noisy stream, whirled and twirled like kites in the sky. The next thing I remember was sitting on the white leather bench with a glass of water in my hand. The stream and the stones were back in place, looking tranquil and zen-like. A slight breeze in the alley made the leaves of the sakura tree shiver delicately.

Tomoko was dead. My brain kept repeating it like a mantra. She was gone. Not gone away for a holiday or moved house, gone as in gone-never-to-come-back. I would never hear her slightly scratchy voice on the phone asking me what I was doing the following day. I would never walk out of the metro into the sunlight and see her waiting for me. I would never again feel the excitement of walking by her side. I stared at the emptiness of the zen garden and felt intimate with it, as if we were now connected.

"Are you all right?" I became aware of the concierge staring worriedly at me. "Shall I bring you some more water?"

"No, no. I am sorry to trouble you like this," I said, getting up to go.

"I am sorry I didn't realise you didn't know," he apologised. "Mr Yamada said that someone would be coming to pick up her things today and I was to hand over the keys. I thought that person was you."

I knew he was wondering who I was and how it was possible for me, her friend, to remain unaware that she was dead, so I hurried to explain. "I was in hospital, giving birth, and then I was busy with my baby. When she didn't return my calls I got worried. So I decided to come and see her."

"I see." He nodded. His body relaxed a little.

When I said nothing but remained where I was in front of him, he took pity on me and broke into speech again. "Ohara-san was such a beautiful young woman. We were all shocked. Mr Yamada especially, he really was crazy about her." He shook his head. "Do you know he hasn't let anyone touch her things till now? He would let himself into the apartment and just sit there, sometimes for just a few minutes, sometimes for an hour or more. Can you imagine, for a busy *shyachyo* like him with thousands of people working under him to grieve for so long? Anyone could see that she was special though, and what a beauty. I just don't understand why she had to..." he stopped, looking at me anxiously.

"I don't understand either. What happened?"

"Threw herself in front of a train, on the Keio Inokashira line, somewhere near Hachioji."

"Hachioji? But that's miles from here."

Because he was talking to another young woman and a friend of the deceased girl, the concierge talked far more openly than he should have. "I can't understand it either," he said, shaking his head sadly. "She must have fallen for a married man. What a pity to waste herself on one of those when there was nothing Yamada-san would not have given her. If she had wanted to go to Paris, he would have taken her to Paris. If she had wanted a new fur coat, he would have given it to her."

My entire body froze. So Tomoko had been the girlfriend of a rich old businessman. She hadn't been going to an office for a long time. She had been living up there in the sky, in a cage made of glass, very luxurious and beautiful perhaps, but a cage none too different from mine.

I laughed out loud, a hard unnatural sound. The concierge stopped midsentence, incomprehension on his face.

Quickly I composed myself and smiled at him apologetically. "I'm sorry. I... I just can't take it all in. She came to see me in the hospital right after I had my baby, that was the last time I saw her."

"Where did you have your baby?" The concierge smiled. Talk of babies reassured him.

"In Seibu Byoin, Mejiro," I answered, lying. Seibu Hospital was where I had been born, not my daughter. Suddenly I had an idea. I placed my hand on the concierge's arm.

"Please," I said, "do you think you could take me up there, to her apartment? I lent her a jacket once, it's... my husband bought it for me and he keeps asking me why I don't wear it."

The concierge pulled back. I could see the refusal forming in his face. But it was my last chance to learn Tomoko's secrets. I simply had to see where she had lived.

"Please..." I said, putting out my hand with the marriage band sitting on the ring finger.

His eyes went to the ring and he hesitated. I let my hand fall lightly onto his arm. Then I let some tears slip out of my eyes. His resistance faded. I could feel it in the way his arm went limp under my hand so that instead of me holding on to him, I was now holding his arm up.

"All right. But you will have to be quick and make no mess, mind you. Just take what is yours and leave everything else exactly the way it was."

"Of course, I understand. Thank you," I said gratefully.

His mind made up, he showed me cordially to the elevator. "It's on the eleventh floor," he said.

I was going to see Tomoko's apartment. I could hardly believe my luck.

The concierge kept his back to me in the elevator and when we arrived he handed me the key and pointed down the hall. "Number 1106 right down the corridor there. Remember to turn the key twice clockwise." I thanked him again and waited till the door of the elevator closed once more before going down the hall.

The corridor was carpeted in brown and grey geometric designs. The walls were a lighter grey, with a touch of blue in them. The overall impression the corridor gave was of masculine seriousness. I had no experience of a building with many apartments like this one. I wondered about the other people who lived in the building. Had they known Tomoko? Were any of them her friends? Lovers? I wanted to knock on the doors I was passing and ask. But the corridor seemed somehow deserted and unlived in, as if there could be no-one living behind those doors for the doors themselves were only pasted onto a blank wall. Such was the silence of that corridor. I imagined Tomoko walking down it, staring at the doors. Did she hate the brown carpet? Did she ever want to scream just to see if anyone would open their doors?

At last I was in front of 1106. My hand trembled as I inserted the key. The air around the door smelled of tobacco and coffee, sugar and soya sauce. The key turned smoothly in the lock and the door sprung open. I hesitated, half expecting someone to shout at me for breaking in. Then I was inside. The curtains were drawn and it was so dark I couldn't make out very much, just the solid shapes of sofas and a table. But I could feel the sadness, maybe Tomoko's, maybe the old man Yamada's, imprinted on the place.

My hand found the light switch and the lights came on. A large, airy room revealed itself, decorated in the contemporary modern style in boldly contrasting blacks and whites. There was a large state-of-the-art television screen on one wall. A white fluffy rug, obviously expensive, was spread in front of the expensive black leather sofa. On top of the rug was a glass table with chrome legs. It was heavy with fashion magazines. Above the television was a bookshelf in black wood. It was filled with expensive-looking books on fashion and design. The two long-necked floor lamps beside the sofa and armchair were also modern looking, clearly imported from Europe and very expensive. But where was Tomoko in all this? I wondered. I tried to imagine her walking up and down Aoyama, choosing the furniture. But I knew it wasn't her who had done it but some expensive designer. I became angry. I had been feeling so happy that I had managed to get into her apartment and now I felt cheated. Even in death, Tomoko was managing to hide her real face from me.

I looked around. Three doors led out of the large living area. The two doors on the right were closed. But to the left, a half-open door revealed a set of gleaming white cupboards and a built-in oven in stainless steel. The kitchen. People often overlooked their kitchens. Perhaps I would find something there?

At first I was disappointed. Everything looked brand new.

The oven was German, a Braun. The sink and the counter opposite were also clean and unmarked. I opened a cupboard and gasped at the collection of fine cutlery. What would happen to all those expensive things, I wondered. The ghost of a laugh began building inside me. Would Yamada-san give them to the next girlfriend?

The fridge, all chrome and shiny, looked new as well. Pasted on the door were notices for swimming lessons, a health club membership renewal, and a few postcards from Europe. I opened the fridge. The shelves were empty. I opened the vegetable tray and it too was empty. Then I opened the freezer door and found only ice and vodka. Next I opened the main section again and began checking the compartments on the door. Inside the butter compartment was a box containing injections and vials marked insulin. So Tomoko's boyfriend Mr Yamada had an insulin problem. I wanted to laugh, a picture of Tomoko playing nurse and shooting insulin into her lover's flabby arm flashing before my eyes.

At last I went to the small kitchen table by the window and, feeling like I had come to the end of the road, I sat down. Then I noticed that the table had lots of yellow stains, the kind made by unextinguished cigarette butts. Aha! I thought, at last. I ran my fingers over the scars on the table as if they were a message. A new image bloomed in my mind—of Tomoko alone at night, smoking cigarette after cigarette as she listened to the radio and flipped through fashion magazines. This picture, I knew, was real.

But still I was not satisfied. What was this Yamada-san like? Was he fat? Was he bald with brown age spots on his face? After a while I headed for Tomoko's bedroom. I hoped there would be at least one photo of the two of them there.

But here again I was disappointed. For the bedroom looked

just like a hotel room—all made up and waiting for a new guest. Either the person who had cleaned up the apartment after her death had made sure that all personal photos had been removed or else there had been none. I stared hard at the room. The black and white theme was in evidence here as well—in the big round double bed covered in black satin sheets embroidered with white roses and the black and white spotted carpet. A sexy black and white photograph of a nude woman hugging a serpent hung on the wall opposite the bed. Behind the bed was a walk-in closet and one entire wall of the bedroom was also devoted to cupboards. I switched off the electric lights and opened the curtains instead. Then I lay down on Tomoko's bed and closed my eyes tightly, trying to imagine them together in that bed. How did she do it? I wondered. Did she, had she loved him? When I opened my eyes, I was seeing what Tomoko must have seen every morning and the view took my breath away. I could see all of Tokyo right up to Shinjuku and the Tokyo metropolitan government building. My eyes embraced the city. I felt as if I owned it. How could one kill oneself when one owned such a view? My anger at Tomoko welled up again. I wanted to hurt her, to burn her house down, to scratch out her eyes. But Tomoko was not there. She would never call me again, never wave her magic wand and lift me out of myself. Slowly the tears began, real tears this time. Bitter tears—for the person they were meant to hurt wasn't there. I turned my back to the window and curled into a tiny ball, my body shaking like a leaf.

When at last I could cry no more, my eyes went to the cupboard and I got off the bed to open the cupboard doors. Clothes came tumbling out like eager pets demanding to be taken for a walk. I stared at them for a full minute—La Perla underwear, Prada skirts, Dior blouses, some still with the tags on them—and slowly the heavy feeling inside me began to lighten. At last I had found her. I could feel her impatient touch. It was as if she had just dressed and gone out for a walk. And when she'd returned she'd just stuffed the things back inside. Clothes were crumpled into careless little bundles and stuffed inelegantly into the shelves—expensive clothes, cheap clothes, dirty and clean clothes. I bent down and picked up a shirt and began folding it—first in half as we had been taught in grade school, then the sleeves and then the rest. When it was done I placed it carefully in the cupboard. Before I knew it I had started organizing the cupboard just as I would have done if Tomoko was alive. I began to comment on the clothes, as if Tomoko was sitting in the other room flipping through one of her fashion magazines.

I don't know how long I spent arranging Tomoko's cupboards but suddenly the impatient ring of the telephone brought me back to the present. Without thinking I picked it up. It was the concierge. "Are you still there?" he asked grumpily. "You will have to leave now. Please return the keys on your way out," he ordered.

"I was just leaving," I lied. Quickly I stuffed the remaining clothes back in the cupboard the way Tomoko would have done and closed the doors. I was about to leave when I remembered my story of the coat I'd lent. So, in order not to arouse the concierge's suspicions, I dashed into the walk-in closet and grabbed the first black coat that came to my hands. Only later did I look at the label. It was a Burberry, a rather expensive one, hundred per cent cashmere.

On the way out of the door, a small pile of mail caught my eye. I bent down to see if there were any magazines or coupons in there. A black postcard with the word "SALE" printed in big gold letters caught my eye. I grabbed it and quickly read the information on the back—Secret Sale, up to 70% off on big European brands. I almost screamed in excitement. I looked at the date and realised the sale was today and that it had already begun three hours ago. I went through the rest of the mail quickly and found two more such postcards—one for Dolce & Gabbana and another for an Issey Miyake sale, which I quickly slipped into my purse.

"Thank you, Tomo-chan," I whispered as I gently shut the door. The apartment seemed to heave a sigh of relief—a place for the dead, wanting only to be left in peace.

People say that the line between life and death is a very clear one, life is life and death is death and the two can never meet. But I think that actually the two live side by side in the same body. One can be alive on the outside—eating, drinking, working—and still feel dead inside. When my husband took me to a priest to cure me of my evil desires I asked the priest how it was possible to be alive on the outside and dead on the inside. And he said that it was possible because sometimes the soul died but the mind didn't realise it and so it told the body to keep on living. When the concierge told me of Tomoko's death I thought that my life too had ended. Not the dead kind of end like Tomoko but the other kind where the soul dies first.

But here again, Tomoko proved to be a true friend. The sale postcards were her last gift, an invitation to keep on 100 per cent living. As soon as I saw them there in the apartment I knew they were there for me.

When I got downstairs I gave the keys back to the concierge. He gave me a hard look but said nothing. I could tell he regretted having given me the keys. Then I was on the street again, and the noise of the traffic, air-conditioners, car wheels, three different kinds of pop music, embraced me. The veil of death slipped off my shoulders and I felt very alive. I took out the card and read the magic words again: "Family Sale". The word "Family" glowed warmly under my fingers. I was going to meet my family. That is how I felt.

As soon as I got off the train at Gotanda, I saw a group of middle-aged women reading a sign. They had large bags under their arms, Gucci or Louis Vuitton, and they looked happy and carefree—like girls on a holiday. But none of them were beautiful like Tomoko. They looked more like me, but a good ten years older. I immediately knew they were going where I was going and so without bothering to read the sign, I followed them. We crossed the busy main street and walked down a slightly narrower arterial road, and at the end of it we turned left, into a grey office building with no signs whatsoever. I hesitated for a second when I saw them enter. I pulled out my card and looked at the address. 10-2-34 Gotanda. World Trade Center Building. I read the name over the entrance. This was it.

Inside the building, beside the elevator I was relieved to see a small sign with "Family Sale, 5th floor" written in hasty letters. The group of women I had been following had already been swallowed by the previous elevator which was slowly working its way up the floors to the tenth and last floor. When at last it began to make its way back down, I almost cried with joy.

The elevator was gigantic, with room for at least fifteen, but by the time it arrived there were double the number of people waiting for it. As I was one of the first, I was able to get a place inside. The elevator filled up, mostly with smartly dressed older women, but there were a few men too and some glamorous young mothers with babies strapped to their chests or in strollers. The atmosphere was tense, like the start of a race or an examination.

I was filled with a strange combination of excitement and nervousness. I had no idea what would be waiting for me on the other side of those steel doors when we reached the fifth floor. So how could I possibly compete with the well-dressed horde?

The doors opened and in front of us was a white desk with a big sign saying "family sale" and an arrow pointing to the right. I began to feel excited. Behind the desk, a polite salesgirl looked at our cards and gave each of us a suitcase-sized plastic bag. I looked at the ugly bag, so different from the elegant ones they gave you in shops and felt sure that I had been tricked. I would have left if it hadn't been for the way the others waited so happily to be let inside. Every few minutes the white warehouse-style double doors opened and a few people came out carrying large white paper bags and looking satisfied. As soon as they left, a tremor went through those who waited. Sure enough, a few seconds later, the doors opened again and a few lucky ones were let inside. My excitement began to build. Was heaven on the other side? I felt sure it was. A heaven of beautiful clothes.

Twenty minutes later, it was my turn to enter. The shiny metal doors opened, the man at the door smiled and nodded at me. I walked hesitantly through the doors. As soon as they closed behind me I stopped, my mouth a giant O of surprise. For what met my eyes was nothing like I had imagined.

Instead of the neat rows of clothes hanging in racks, nice music, and friendly well-dressed salesgirls, I found a giant hall that resembled Tsukiji fish market. People in knee-length white coats, like those worn by hospital staff or factory workers, were carrying wheelbarrows full of clothes to and fro. There were clothes everywhere—bursting from gigantic aluminum hangers, in untidy bundles on hastily erected tables, in hurricane mounds on the floor. People were clustered around the hangers and tables like so many ants around sugar, their hands disappearing into the piles of clothes and coming out with clumps of crumpled cloth which they stuffed hastily into sheer plastic sacks. The tubelights did nothing to enhance the beauty of the clothes and yet my eyes were dazzled. Because I wasn't looking at the lights, I was looking at the women.

I knew the look on their faces intimately. I had felt it inside me any number of times, that hunger. The women were in a feeding frenzy. Quietly and methodically, with utmost concentration, they picked their way through the bundles of clothing the way starving animals gnawed at the carcasses of their prey.

I joined them, filled with the same determination I saw in their faces. Quickly I sorted through the bundles of clothes, dropping anything that looked remotely wearable into my giant plastic bag. It filled up rapidly, getting almost too heavy to hold, but still I kept going—picking, picking, picking—like all the other women were.

At last I was done. Clothes hung from every part of my body. I was a walking clothes rack. But I was happy.

I joined the long line of women waiting to go into the makeshift changing room. It took forty five minutes to get inside. When I entered I got another surprise. There were no private cabins like in the department stores. Instead, forty full-length mirrors were lined up back-to-back and in front of each was a half-naked woman with her plastic sac and clothes scattered at her feet. The mirrors made the room seem even more crowded than it actually was. And the noise was incredible. For having made their choices the women were relaxed and ready to laugh and chat. Clothes and bags lay everywhere and the place was a mess.

The chaos looked oddly familiar. Then I realised why—it looked like the inside of a normal Japanese home. A sense of homecoming swept over me. At last I had found the place to which I belonged. And it was not the fancy department stores of Ginza and Omotesando, it was here in the glorious disorder of this warehouse changing room in a forgotten part of the city. My body filled with joy, my head grew light and suddenly I knew that my future was full of beautiful things.

The Double Life

After Tomoko's death I began to lead a double life. During the week I would look after my family. I would wake up at 5.45 a.m., prepare breakfast and bentos for my husband and son, wake baby Haruka, feed her, get her dressed, and then wake up my son. I would get Akira dressed and feed and walk him to the local playschool, accompanied by little Haruka in the McLaren. After that I would do the day's shopping and come home via the park so that Haruka could play there for a while. On the way into the house I would pick up the mail, quickly checking for family sale postcards. Then I would bathe, change and feed Haruka and play with her till she grew sleepy. Then, while Haruka slept, I would clean the house and prepare lunch. If I had time leftover, I would read a little. Not books, for I could no longer recognize all the kanji, but women's magazines or Ryu's manga books. When Haruka awoke we would eat and then go to the park. Around 3.30 p.m., we would do another round of shopping and fetch Akira from his kindergarten. In the evening I would bathe and feed the children and read with Akira till bedtime. Most nights I was asleep when my husband would return from office. My other life would begin on the weekends: on Saturday mornings, even before I opened my eyes, my body would feel different—as if someone had rubbed it with snow and a million little eyes had suddenly opened all over my body. Even my breasts would feel different—rounder, tighter, and younger—as if they too knew that it was time for them to be pampered and admired once more. As I would lie with Ryu's heavy foot on my thighs, his arm on my chest, I would plan what I would wear that day. In my mind I would open my secret bags of beautiful clothes, and take them out one by one. I would shake out the creases and look at them with pride, anticipating the joy to come.

Though the sales would only begin at eleven or sometimes even twelve, it was best to get there early and wait in line so that one could be amongst the first to enter. Then one was sure of finding good things. So I would get up early, make breakfast and a cold lunch, and leave the house by nine-thirty. If Ryu was planning to be at home, I would leave him to deal with the children. If he had work or a basketball game, I would leave the children with an obaa-chan. There would have been no children in Tokyo if there hadn't been obaa-chans. In those days there were still quite a few of them around. Now there are almost none. And see how few children there are these days?

By the time I would get to the sale, my body would be on fire—every nerve and muscle stretched tight like a warrior's. My senses would be sharp, the mind focused and alert. Then either I would get into the line or if I was early I would wait in a coffee shop. Had it been you waiting in my place, you would have become impatient. But we are different. We wait patiently because waiting is a pleasure. For waiting does not require us to make any decisions or shoulder any responsibility. While we wait we simply occupy space and disturb no-one.

So I would carry a book or magazine with me, pretend to read, and wait for the doors to open. The waiting would calm me, and prepare me for the electric storm of emotion that was to come.

You raise your eyebrows. How can a sale be such a big

thing, your face says. But have you ever watched the dice rolling and felt that your future happiness depended upon it? That is how I felt every time I went for a family sale. Dice rolled wildly in my head as I passed through the steel doors. I felt the exquisite excitement of the gambler, the lightning streak of anxiety that was also the taste of life stripped of every disguise. I was not only a gambler then but also a hunter, because hunting, I realised, was a form of gambling too. Yes, it is true, because in hunting too there is great risk. You risk your life, not just your money.

You laugh. But I promise you I do not exaggerate. For each time one goes in, one risks coming out unsatisfied. For family sales are for getting rid of things that have not sold in the shops. They are about *nokorimono*, leftovers. Finding something that is your size and looks good on your body amongst the leftovers is not easy. You have to have a lot of luck.

In Japan, to be invited to a family sale you have to fill out a white form with your address and telephone details when you arrive at the reception. Then you will be on the list and will be sent the postcards automatically. But the person behind the reception desk won't give you the form unless you ask for it. And to ask for it you have to know about it. When I went to that first family sale with Tomoko's card I didn't know this. And if it hadn't been for the purest bit of good luck I would never again have been invited to another family sale in my life. But in the elevator going up to the fifth floor I overheard two foreigners talking in English. They were also going to the sale I realised, seeing the card in the taller woman's hand. It is a habit of mine to listen carefully whenever I heard someone speaking English, for my teacher always said that the best way to learn a language was to listen to it.

"You see, Emily, you have to be invited to these sales," the taller one was saying. "So when you get to the reception, say you were invited by your friend and you would like to fill out a form for yourself. The woman will give you a white slip. Take it and write in your name, address and telephone number. Then they will put you on their list and the next time they have a sale they will invite you."

When it was my turn to show my card at the counter I did exactly what the American woman had advised her friend to do. I asked for the form and when it was given to me, I filled it out carefully with my own name and address. I did the same thing at the two other sales and soon the cards began to arrive in my own mail box. Was I not lucky? How else can you explain the coincidence involving the two women in the elevator where they were discussing how the system worked in my presence?

So like a gambler, I too have become superstitious. I read my horoscope in the papers on Friday, I go to the temple and offer prayers for a thousand yen twice a week. I avoid wearing mustard yellow and grey, for twice when I have worn those colours to a sale, I came back with nothing. And as a result, luck is always on my side. I never return empty-handed from a sale. This is not just because I am lucky. I am also a good hunter, a careful hunter. I only go for the best things, for only the best things give lasting pleasure. Tomoko taught me this. Indeed, she prepared me well. On my weekly visits to the shrine, I always say a prayer for her soul.

*

At first I only went to one or two sales every six months, then more and more postcards began to arrive and soon I was going to two-three sales per weekend. I even got to know some of the other ladies and they began to recognize me, nodding to me in the elevator on the way down, asking me if I had found nice things. Sometimes I saw them in the café after the sale and we would talk a little—polite nothings about the sale, the number of people, the discomfort. And underneath the words was the magic lake of companionship, the sense of a shared something, as if we had all been dipping our hands into the same secret life-giving pool.

One day, as I was sitting in a Jonathan's family restaurant, waiting for a sale to open its doors, a strange question blossomed in my mind: what was hell like? I wondered. I stirred in the sugar and smiled into the mud-coloured drink, remembering the old Buddhist story rewritten by Akutagawa which we had all been made to study in school. In the story, hell was depicted as a boiling lake of blood, thick and opaque like the coffee. But my answer, which came to me almost at the same moment, was different. Hell was being without shops and family sales to go to. I thought of Tomoko and my heart went out to her. Wherever her soul was, it was definitely in torment. For what feeling could compete with the exquisite intoxication of shopping? How did Tomoko's spirit-self feel, I wondered, having the desire to buy eating at it and being unable to do anything about it? I finished my coffee quickly, enjoying its bitterness, and went outside and joined the line.

In the time I had been having coffee, the line had grown quite long, and so I had to wait outside the building as the lobby was already full. I sighed silently and wondered if my luck would hold. Issey Miyake sales were very popular and people came in busloads from all over the country. I looked around to see if anyone was watching me, and noticed a tired-looking middle-aged woman staring jealously at my boots. In these lines, we were all watching each other all the time. I saw a woman I recognized from other sales a little in front of me and we nodded at each other. But because the line was especially long, everyone was nervous and kept to themselves.

At last the ushers began to call and the line moved on into the building. By the time I got inside, the hall was crowded and the noise deafening. There must have been at least five hundred people there. But still there remained many clothes. I began my search, moving methodically from one section to the next, starting with the "Pleats please" section which was the most popular and then moving to the more expensive Issey Miyake "Fête" line. If you don't know, "fête" means "party" in French.

It was not long after I had begun the "Fête" range that I saw something I will never forget. Two women grabbed the same Issey Miyake jacket from opposite sides of a clothes rack. They could not see each other. But they could feel the presence of the other through the cloth. Yet neither woman was willing to let go of the jacket. So they just stood there, holding tight and waiting for the other woman to let go. I watched them fascinated. I was not alone. There were others. I wondered which woman would feel the shame first and let go. But neither seemed ready to let the other one get the jacket. Looking at their stony faces, I suddenly lost my desire for shopping. Neither woman was beautiful or young or well-dressed. They were just two middle-aged women living an anonymous life in some Tokyo suburb. I tried to imagine where and when they would wear the jacket each was holding on to so determinedly —at the supermarket maybe, or in their moments of solitude. It came to me in a flash that probably whoever got it in the end would never wear it, that they would do what I did, taking it out from time to time in their heads in that sliver of time that was theirs to dream in. They would think about the jacket as they watched their husbands eat the food they had made without even looking at them once and they would feel happy.

Unable to stop myself I burst into laughter. The two women looked at me simultaneously, anger flaring in their eyes. They both let go of the jacket and moved away to opposite ends of the room. Embarrassed at my lack of control, I too moved away and not long after I left without buying anything at all—for inside me the bubbly intoxication of buying had completely disappeared. But when the next SALE postcard came, the need to buy returned.

A Letter from the Bank

One day I got a letter from the bank. It was a very polite letter, so polite that at first I didn't fully understand what they were trying to tell me. I could have asked Ryu, he worked in a bank, but one of the principal rules of the double life is secrecy. None of my family could know. If I sought Ryu's help I would no longer have had a double life and without it, I believed I would most certainly become part of the living dead. I read the letter several times till its meaning became clear. Did I know, it said, that I had a credit card bill of 215,678 yen while there was only 76,215 yen left in my account? That was the essence of it.

Perhaps if my mother had been around I would have shared the letter with her. Her gift to me was after all at the root of the problem. But not long after she visited me, my mother disappeared. She did it well, closing her bank accounts and selling off all her possessions. Another cheque arrived for me, but this time without a letter from her. I think that she went to live with my brother in America. Maybe she met a nice American and married again. All I know for sure is that the money she sent me was not kimono money, it was her life's savings.

Since the letter from the bank was titled *oshirase* or information, I did nothing about it. Someone at the bank must have made an accounting mistake. I had not bought that much! And even if I had, when last checked, I still had a million and a half in my account. No-one could spend that much money so fast.

And I only bought two or three things each time I went shopping. So I waited for another letter to arrive, apologizing for the mistake and the inconvenience it had caused me.

But no such letter came. A week became two weeks and two weeks became a month. Then the month stretched into four. I almost forgot about the letter. After a month I went back to my sales, happily unaware of the sword that hung over my head.

The call came at eleven-fifteen on a Wednesday morning. I was alone in the house. I had just finished cleaning and was about to begin preparing lunch and even before I picked up I knew it was bad news. No-one called the house in the daytime. My first thought as I rubbed my trembling hands on my apron was that it was Ryu's bank calling because something had happened to Ryu.

"Hello, is Mrs Suzuki Kayo there?"

"Yes, it's Mrs Suzuki speaking."

"This is Takabayashi Kyoko speaking from Sumitomo Bank Credit and Loans Department. If I am not disturbing you, may I talk with you for a few minutes?"

She was so polite I could not refuse even though later I wished I had.

"You are a valued customer of our bank," she began, "and sometime ago we had written to you of a small problem with your account. Did you receive our letter? Are you aware of the problem?"

I should have lied but I could not. So I said, "I did receive something but I couldn't quite understand its meaning so I gave it to my husband." Of course the last part was a lie and I am sure the woman on the other end of the line knew it, for she continued mechanically, "Are you aware that you have an overdraft of 489,327 yen? Your interest-free period will end this coming Monday, and I have been charged with informing you that as of Monday you will be paying sixteen per cent interest on your overdraft. Have you understood?"

I didn't say anything. My brain refused to understand. I heard her sigh impatiently and when I still didn't say anything she repeated her question, "Have you understood? The bank will be charging sixteen per cent interest on your overdraft from Monday onwards. It is in your interest to pay as soon as possible."

"But how... I had three million and a half in my account not so long ago," I finally managed to stammer.

"I don't know about what you had in the past. I am simply informing you of the present situation of your account. Thank you for your time. If you have any further questions, kindly visit your local branch office and speak directly to them. Thank you very much for your time."

And with that she ended the conversation. The message had been delivered. I stared blindly at the telephone in my hand before carefully putting the receiver back onto its cradle. So the letter had not been a mistake. Somehow, in little less than a year I had managed to spend over two million yen. And now it was I who owed the bank money.

All of a sudden, my eyes were drawn to the window. Outside, the weeping cherry blossom had just finished delivering its yearly quota of pink flowers and was now clad in delicate new leaves. I stared at it as if I was seeing it for the first time. Ryu always said that it was the cherry blossom that made him decide to buy the house and so I had decided to hate it. Now I found myself admiring its delicate beauty. On the tip of one branch, a single pink and white blossom remained. My eyes went to the grey stone wall just behind it that separated the house from the cherry tree-lined avenue. The wall had always bothered me because it was made of a kind of grey stone that belonged to pictures of the English countryside rather than Tokyo. Now I found myself examining it in a different way, noticing how solid it was, and how well it guarded us from the prying eyes of our neighbours.

It is in the nature of woman that when faced with a wall, she will find a way to climb over it. I did not panic or cry. For who would have seen me? And what good would it have done anyway? I made my lunch and ate it in silence bite by bite. One fact was clear to me now—I was in debt. I owed the bank close to four hundred thousand. An image of my father lying face down on the ground begging for his life came to me with such force that I almost choked. After his death we had never spoken of him. It was as if he had left for a business trip somewhere. I knew why, of course. Japanese do not talk about shameful things. In fact, I had almost forgotten about him— till now. But all of a sudden the memories came back and I remembered him perfectly, and his shame and mine became one. So I am like my father then, I thought. Strangely, I felt glad. I had always feared I would end up like my mother.

By the time I finished my lunch, my mind was searching and discarding ways out of my situation. I knew my father's story. I knew how interest could pile up, turning a small debt into a Mount Fuji. Had my father's Mount Fuji also begun with a bank? I wondered. I didn't think so.

At that point, if I had been smart, I would have confessed everything to Ryu and asked him to pay. But I was too proud. And also, if I told him, I would have to confess that I hid my mother's money from him, that I opened a separate bank account, and that I spent all the money on clothes for myself when he was killing himself trying to pay off our house loan. I could clearly visualize the look on his face. I closed my eyes so tightly they hurt but I could not squeeze out the picture of Ryu's face. Then and there I decided never to let him find out—no matter what I had to do to get the money. Whatever I did, I would have to do it alone.

For the first time in my life, I spent the rest of the day worrying about money. Our housekeeping money was 160,000 a month. I kept it in a steel safe under our bed. I rushed upstairs and took out the safe. I counted the money inside. Around 90,000 and if I was very careful I could manage on 50,000 till the end of the month. But compared to what I owed, the amount seemed tiny. By three, when it was time to pick up the children I still hadn't decided what to do. I thought about selling my clothes at a pawn shop, but the thought of parting with my beautiful things was too painful. Besides, pawn shops gave next to nothing for used clothes. Even if I sold them all, I reasoned, I would only get twenty or thirty thousand.

If I had been a strong person, I would have gone immediately to sell my clothes and taken the money I received along with the house money and begged the bank to reschedule my loan. Living frugally and not going shopping, I may have been able to pay off the loan, even with the high interest, in a year or so. But the idea of never going to a sale again was too terrible. I would die, I thought, and like all weak people of course, I didn't have the courage to kill myself.

So at quarter to three I got onto my electric mamachari and went to pick up Haruka who was playing at a friend's house. In front of the station, beside the Pink Pelican pachinko parlour, I was almost run over by a black Crown saloon—the kind used only by the Imperial family and the Yakuza. The car screeched to a halt and two young men in expensive clothes leapt out.

"Are you all right?" I was asked in a thick Kansai accent.

"Yes, yes. I am fine." The bicycle had fallen on top of me and from the car an ice-cold voice barked an order: "Pick up the goddamn bike and get her onto the pavement."

I looked up but the man's face was shadowed and I couldn't tell if the owner of that voice was young or old. The two Yakuza picked up my bike and helped me to the pavement. From the interior of the Pink Pelican parlour two young women came rushing out. They took charge of me instantly, shooing the men away. One parked my bicycle and the other took me to the washroom to tidy up. They were so nice and warm that I felt certain they weren't Japanese. I remembered reading somewhere that all pachinko parlours were actually owned by the Korean mafia. That would explain why the girls were so pretty. They were probably Korean and all used those special Korean cosmetics made of snake venom and frog saliva and things. When I came out, they had tea ready for me in the office. While the noise inside the parlour had been deafening, inside the office it was quiet. Through a glass window I could see the players at the machines. On an adjacent wall there was a series of small circuit TV screens showing the inside of the men's and ladies' toilets, the cashier area, the lockers and other slot machines. On the other wall was a Chinese scroll painting and a large fish tank filled with golden-and-orange-coloured goldfish.

Because I have long held the belief that pachinko parlours are for weak people, I had never been inside one and so I stared curiously at the people playing the machines and was surprised by how normal they looked. It was difficult to put them into any category because there were all sorts in there—young people, high-school students, older men in suits, older women in unfashionable clothes, obaa-chans and oji-chans in tracksuit bottoms, young men in fashionable denims, young office women in typical formal attire, and of course some housewives in beige raincoats. I was surprised to see the raincoats, for it had not rained all day and wasn't expected to rain till 6 p.m. Then it came to me that they had brought their raincoats because they were planning to remain in the parlour till nightfall.

How do all those people spend their entire day in such a noisy place? I wondered. I turned to my two hosts. "Do you know all the people who come to your place?" I asked. "Are they from around here?"

The taller, not-so-pretty one replied. "Some are regular customers," she said, "some aren't."

"You see that man there with the bowler hat," the other girl said, coming right up behind me and pointing to the far right corner of the picture window, "he's from Tokyo Minato Ku but he comes here every day."

"Every day?" I could hardly believe my ears. The man looked like a rich businessman. He had to be rich if he lived in Minato Ku. "Yes, he comes at ten and he stays till four 4.45 p.m. Every day," she answered matter-of-factly.

"But it's so noisy! How do the older people stand the noise?" I asked.

The pretty one shrugged. "They don't seem to be bothered by it."

"Maybe their houses are too quiet," the not-so-pretty one added. I finished my tea and stood up.

"Thank you for taking care of me," I said formally. "I am sorry to have disturbed you."

"Not at all, please come again, anytime," they both said casually. The prettier one handed me my coat. "A cashmere Burberry, wow, you must be rich," she remarked. She looked hard at me again, as if she was seeing me for the first time and her hand came out to touch my dress. As I was feeling so depressed I had put on one of my favourites, a Max Mara dress in wine red velvet. With it I wore an Armani jacket of navy blue. "You have beautiful clothes. And they make you look so pretty. If you worked here, you would surely bring in many, many customers."

"Oh yes, they would love you," the other one agreed, coming closer.

"Well, thank you. But both of you are extremely pretty, much prettier and younger than I am," I said, laughing uncomfortably. In my mind I thought that they were most certainly Korean. No Japanese would be so rude.

"I really have to go," I said stiffly.

"Don't be offended," the taller one said, "we didn't mean to make you uncomfortable. It is just that you are so well-dressed and classy. We never see people like you... except in magazines."

The prettier one nodded, adding, "Please let us show you around? Would you like to play the machines a little?"

"I didn't bring any money," I said without thinking. The next moment I regretted my words for they immediately said in unison, "Please do us the favour of letting us give you some balls for free."

"No, no. I must go and pick up my daughter," I said weakly. The two young women smiled understandingly.

A Very Sticky Thing

Buddhist texts say that desire is the root of all our problems. They are right. If one could only separate people from their desire, those same people who flock to the pachinko parlours night and day would go home and live a peaceful life, not troubling family and friends and wasting their hard-earned money. But only the Buddha and a few others were able to separate themselves from desire. For desire is a very sticky thing. If this were fiction and not the real story of my life, at this point I would write that instead of shopping I got hooked on to pachinko, got even more into debt and ended my life the way Tomoko did, under the steel wheels of a train. Or, if it were a happy novel, I would say that I won a lot of money at pachinko, cashed it in, repaid my debt and lived happily ever after. Neither would be true.

I hated the little rolling silver balls from the very beginning. And I hate them still. The balls are blind, they are without feeling, without mercy. Sometimes they pretend to be your friend but actually they are laughing at you. That first day when I was handed a basket for my winnings and a bag of silver balls to play with, I didn't believe that I could win. I didn't even want to win. Yet I did win. I won a lot. I don't really know what I did or how it happened but suddenly every time the balls stopped spinning more silver balls poured out of the bottom of the machine. Soon there was so much it began to overflow onto the floor. Other players stopped their games to watch me. I felt strange. But there was nothing I could do. The machine seemed to have decided to make me a winner. The sound of balls rolling across the floor brought one of the Koreans and she clapped and said, "Lucky *desu*, lucky" over and over.

When I encashed my winnings, the Korean girls seemed slightly disappointed even though they remained polite and were quick to point out how lucky I'd been. I thanked them and left, not bothering to count what I had made. I wasn't going to go back. The street, though lined with restaurants and bars, was an oasis of peace after the noise and chaos of the parlour. I was happy to be in the real world again.

But in reality my happiness had another source. Though I didn't realise it then, it was the pachinko that had made me happy again. The machines had let me win, and so when I came back onto the street I felt like a winner again. In front of my family I was able to pretend perfectly and dinner went smoothly. After I had put Haruka to bed, the three of us, Akira, Ryu and I watched a television serial together, one of those NHK samurai dramas they are always showing. And in the middle of the serial, just as the hero is forced to run away from his home and loses the woman he loves and becomes a ronin, I felt a sudden surge of hope. Maybe I was like the hero of the story. Terrible things happened to me because I was somebody special. Strength surged through me. Tomorrow I would call the bank and put an end to my problems.

But the next day, once I had the house to myself, my confidence melted away. What was I—just another stupid housewife, in debt because she was too weak to control her desires? I felt dirty, ashamed, as if I hadn't bathed in a week. I felt terrified too—that my husband would find out. There was no way he would forgive me. My hand began to tremble and the cup I was holding fell and broke into pieces. I didn't do anything for a long time, staring at the broken pieces like a fortune teller looking at the future. Then I remembered the money I'd made and went upstairs to find it. It was still in my purse, a thick roll of yen. I counted it—45,000. Not a lot of money but not an insignificant amount either. Quickly I did the calculations. I needed 489,327. If I took 55,000 from the housekeeping money I could give the bank 100,000 straight away. And if I ran out of money before the end of the month I would ask Ryu for a little. He would not suspect. It had happened before.

I bent down and picked up the broken cup. I would go to the bank the following day, I decided.

But the next day when I woke up, my courage had deserted me and so it was only two weeks later, when the feeling of unease had increased to the point that I could no longer sleep, that I finally went to the bank.

I had only ever been to a bank once, the time I opened my account. At the time there had been only men in the bank and the man assigned to me had been kind, helpful and polite. This time, the customer service agent was a girl half my age and fat, with teeth rotted by sugar. "Sorry to keep you waiting," she said automatically, "how can I help you?" Because I was staring at her teeth I could not immediately reply. In my generation only a few of us had bad teeth. Nowadays of course you will find almost as many dental clinics as hairdressers in Tokyo but in those days it was different, and she was the first Japanese I was seeing with such bad teeth that I cannot forget.

"What can I do for you?" she asked as I stared at her rudely.

"Uh, oh. I came about my account," I stammered, quickly looking down.

"Your account number?" she asked.

I gave it to her hesitantly and she typed the number into the computer in a businesslike fashion, the crystals in her beautifully painted nails flashing as she typed. When she finally turned back to me, her manner had changed completely. "You are in overdraft," she stated baldly. "What are you planning to do about it?"

"Yes, yes, I am so sorry. I didn't realise," I said embarrassedly, shrinking into my chair.

"Have you come to pay us back?" Her voice rang out like a temple bell and I looked around worriedly, wondering if others had heard her. But everyone was carrying on with their business as if nothing had happened.

"Yes, yes. That is exactly why I have come," I told her hastily, opening my purse and taking out my roll of money.

She took the money without comment and got up. "One moment please," she said automatically. Her politeness was like her make-up, too visible and badly applied.

When she came back, there was a man with her. I stood up, relieved. At last someone I could talk to.

"Mrs Suzuki. A pleasure to meet you. Maruyama Kenji is my name," the man said, handing me his business card. I felt strange being addressed by my maiden name. But that was the name I had given the bank when I had started the account.

"*Yoroshiku onegaishimasu*," I replied, inclining my head graciously. The man was so polite it was difficult not to be.

"I am the person who handles your account here at this bank," he said cheerfully. "Please come with me."

I tucked his card into my handbag, and followed him across the room to a quiet sunny corner by the window where three sofas were placed around a table with a miniature bonsai set in the centre. He fetched me a cup of tea and sat down beside me. Then he thanked me formally for my visit to the bank and for the hundred thousand repayment and then asked politely about my health and my family. After a pause, with a light embarrassed cough he introduced the real subject of our conversation. But since he did it so politely I felt no embarrassment at all. "And what would you like to do about the rest of the money you owe us?"

"I will repay it of course," I said.

"Of course," he agreed.

"All of it," I added. "But it's just that right now I cannot pay it back immediately."

Maruyama Kenji nodded understandingly. "That is not a problem, you can pay in installments," he said.

"I can give you 50,000 a month," I promised boldly.

He smiled broadly. "That is wonderful, even at sixteen per cent interest you will be in the clear in less than two years. Then we will be able to give you a new credit card."

"Interest? But... I am just a poor housewife, not a business, how can you make me pay interest?" I burst out angrily.

He smiled again, a smile of practised regret. "Yes, we understand, that is why we waited six months before charging interest. I am so sorry. But you see we are a bank, not a charity." Then his smile changed. "I will have to ask you for your cheque book and card. We cannot issue you a new credit card till you have cleared your debt, but if you can wait for a few minutes while I fill out a form, I can give you a new cheque book for your new overdraft account. That way you will still have access to some money in case you need it."

I shook my head. "No thank you, I don't need any money," I said firmly, standing up. "I have disturbed you enough."

Maruyama-san looked embarrassed and accompanied me wordlessly to the exit. I walked stiffly in front of him, furious.

He accompanied me down the steps to the street and when I turned to him to say goodbye, he said, "Mrs Suzuki, I am so sorry. I wish I could have done something but I am just an employee here. I have to follow the rules."

"You don't have to apologise," I said stiffly, "you are only the postman."

He gave an embarrassed smile and, looking quickly around to see if there was anyone nearby, dropped his voice to a whisper and said urgently, "If you do not want to pay so much interest, I have a suggestion." He took a card out of his pocketbook and handed it to me. "Contact these people for a loan. They will give you a cheaper rate and so you can pay us immediately and then pay them off more slowly—and it will cost you less."

I looked at the card suspiciously. "Why are you doing this?" I asked bluntly.

He answered calmly as if he had made up his mind. "Because I don't think the bank should be charging people like yourself such high rates of interest. I want to help you."

Reassured, I put the card into my handbag. The man had a heart. The world of bankers wasn't a wholly evil place after all.

"Their office is in Gotanda. Go and see them now," he advised. "They can make a wire transfer to us today, and then your account won't become an overdraft account at all. This will let you hold on to your credit card also."

I shook my head. "I don't want a credit card ever again."

Full of hope, I went to the address he'd given me in Gotanda. Because of the many sales I had been to in the area, I thought I knew it quite well. But when I reached the address he had given me I was sure I'd made a mistake. For the building was a rundown five-storey tenement from the fifties. The walls were grey with age and eighties pollution. They looked as if they hadn't been painted since the building was built. Only the reinforced steel doors on each apartment looked new. Beside each door was a mean little window covered in frosted glass and wire mesh. Above the windows were a bird's nest of wires from which more wires led to the neighbouring apartments. The whole place smelled of stale food, and broken dreams. This was no office building, this was a place where people hid from the world. I looked at the card doubtfully but the address was correct. And so I went to inspect the letter-boxes and there I found it: "Sun Rise Loan and Investments" written in newly painted English letters.

Had the office been on the third or even second floor I would probably not have gone in. But Sun Rise Loan and Investments was only two doors away from where I stood in front of the letter-boxes. As soon as I rang the bell a young woman wearing lots of make-up and a short tight dress opened the door. Her hair was dyed a dark blond and permed into Marilyn Monroe curls and her nails were encrusted with Swarovski crystals of different colours. Gold flashed at her throat and on her wrist was a Rolex watch, fake or not I could not tell, but what I was sure of was that she, too, did not belong to the building. "Yes? What can I do for you?" she asked disinterestedly. Something in the way she looked at me made me certain she was not Japanese. It was too curious, too openly calculating. The thought came to me that there was no politeness in her. Wordlessly I showed her the card in my hand.

"Who sent you?" she asked suspiciously.

"Mr Maruyama," I stuttered.

"Follow me," she said, preceding me into the room. I looked at her shoes. They were Pradas. Inside the office was a one-room tunnel apartment with a little kitchenette to the right and a minuscule toilet to the left. A sink was stuck onto the wall beside the toilet. It contained the remains of a hastily eaten meal. Like an animal who had just been led into a cage, I looked around warily. The room was a mess. Cheap filing cabinets lined the walls and files had been stuffed into these until the doors themselves could no longer close. More files sat on the floor, and buried beneath yet more paper was a computer. I could see no printer at all but at the time I was so confused by the place that I didn't really look for it. Near the window at the rear of the room there were two desks facing each other. I noticed them because unlike the rest of the room, they were completely free of anything. A man was seated on the edge of the left-hand desk, his back to the room, talking on the phone. The woman guided me to the other desk and bade me, sit down. "What kind of loan will you be wanting?" she asked.

"I... I am not sure," I stammered, wanting to leave. "Just a small loan."

She sniffed but didn't reply. We both looked towards the man and waited for him to tell us what to do. Even as he continued to talk on the phone, the man turned around and flashed me a gold-capped smile.

I knew then that I had been led into a trap. For though the man was dressed in an expensive banker's suit, his face was not the refined face of an educated man. A low forehead, a broad nose that looked broken in at least two places, small, yellow eyes, and a big heavy jaw rather like a gorilla's met my horrified eyes. And he wore no tie. Even without knowing what kind of shoes he wore I knew at once that I was facing the same kind of people my father had faced twenty-five years earlier.

At that moment I should have got up, made some excuse and run away. But fear takes away not only the mind but also the capacity to move. "*Jya... mata*," he told the person on the other end of the line familiarly and disconnected.

"What can I do for you?" he asked me in a thick Osaka accent.

Nothing, I wanted to reply, you can do nothing for me. But I was so frightened that I could say nothing. So after a minute's silence, he spoke instead. "Are you Mrs Suzuki? Maruyama-san called and told me about your little problem. My name is Yamashita." He eyed my breasts in a detached but appreciative way.

I shivered and wished I had a coat which I could clutch around my neck. But since I was wearing only a dress I could do nothing except look down, feeling utterly humiliated. This gave him a good look at my breasts. "I would be happy to help a beautiful woman like you," he said.

I looked up angrily. "How much do you need?" he asked in a more businesslike tone. The lump in my throat prevented me from speaking, so he answered for me after a slight pause, "You owe the bank 389,287—we can round off the number to 400,000 so that you have a little to celebrate with." He clapped his hands together looking delighted, "So 400,000—would that be enough for you or shall we round it off to 500,000?"

I saw nothing to celebrate in my situation. All I wanted was to leave as quickly as possible.

"400,000 is fine, thank you," I said politely.

"Wonderful." He smiled like a shark who had just eaten and nodded at the woman who suddenly reappeared at his side. She had a sheaf of papers in her arms which she put before him and quickly melted into the shadows once more.

"Fill in your name, husband's name, address and date of birth please," he instructed as if I could not read the form for myself.

"My husband's name? I'm not..." I wanted to say I wasn't

113

married but the words wouldn't come out of my mouth. I was superstitious about lies. They had a way of coming true.

Mr Yamashita reached across and patted my hand reassuringly. "It's just a formality. You see, every loan needs a guarantor," he explained, "...in case you cannot pay us back. This can be either a parent, a sibling or a husband. In your case I assumed you would want to put your husband's name. But don't worry, we will not involve him at all. This remains between you and me, as you are the sole person responsible for paying back your loan."

I didn't want to give him my husband's name and if I had been a strong person, I would have walked out at that moment. But I am not strong; I am just a woman used to taking orders from men and so I meekly gave him my husband's name, and filled out the rest of the form. Then I signed it and he stamped it with their seal.

He looked over the papers briefly and handed them to the other woman. "All right then. Congratulations. I have the details of the bank and will wire them the money straight away." He opened his wallet and took out 11,000 yen. "And this is yours. Don't worry about the change," he said, standing up. "Now my colleague will explain the rest to you."

A human being's moods are like leaves blown by the wind. When I left the loan shark's office I was relieved but scared. On the way to the train I grew angry and cursed the banker Maruyama who had suggested I go there. But somehow thinking of the nice Mr Maruyama as a criminal didn't feel right and I began to argue with myself in his favour. After all, thanks to him, I had resolved my problem without having to go to my husband. I calculated that if I paid a minimum of 30,000 yen each month, the rate of interest on the loan remained at 6.5 per cent a month, 9.5 per cent less than what the bank would charge me. However, if I could not pay 30,000 yen each month, the interest rate jumped to 25 per cent a month. But that didn't worry me. I could easily pay 30,000 yen from the house money Ryu gave me. In around two years I would be free.

And so by the time the train arrived at my station I had even mentally composed a nice letter of thanks to Mr Maruyama. In the street I saw some fresh chicken skewers being sold on an old-fashioned handcart by a young hippie. I stopped in front of the cart, feeling suddenly guilty. How long was it since I had bought my family chicken skewers, I wondered. I could not remember. That evening the atmosphere at the dinner table became almost festive when my family saw the chicken skewers. Only Ryu was a little suspicious and remarked, "You act like you won the lottery today. What's the matter?"

"Nothing's the matter," I replied, not looking at him, then added, "I am happy that's all. You just never notice."

It was a mean remark but Ryu's expression didn't change. "I am glad that you are happy," he said quietly.

Shame filled my heart and I got up and hid myself in the kitchen, pretending to tidy up. It was easy to blame my husband for everything. In the middle of the night, inside my secret garden, I had thought plenty of terrible things about him. But I had always managed to keep my feelings to myself. Why had it suddenly come out? I vowed to myself it would never happen again.

The Difficult Art of Being Boring

My days resumed their placid flow. On the outside nothing had changed. But on the inside, in my heart and mind, everything was different. My simple housewife's days glowed and pulsated with energy—for my heart had changed, and so everything else had changed too. Because I had nearly lost them, my family, my house, my life had become precious to me.

And so, for the first time, I found myself liking my boring little life—my children who were growing up, my husband who was not too successful but not unsuccessful either, not handsome but not ugly either, not rich but not poor either. I began to feel proud of my not-so-little, difficult-to-clean house facing the avenue lined with cherry blossoms, my kitchen with its many dead angles where neither cupboard nor refrigerator would fit, my pocket handkerchief-sized garden which burst into life every spring. I even began to enjoy the cleaning liquids—each with their own special smells—that I used each day.

Overnight, I went from wanting to escape my life to being attached to it. And the very same things that had once felt like giant chains tying me to a living death became like offerings made upon the altar of my happiness. I became a different person. I cooked proper meals for Ryu and the children and woke up at four-thirty to make them elegant bentos. I did everything magazines like Fujingaho told me to do in order to be a good wife. I dressed carefully, made sure my hair always looked freshly washed and blow dried and my nails were painted. I never went out without a designer handbag so that my husband would not be shamed in front of the neighbours. I learnt to bake American cakes and offered them regularly to my husband's American colleagues as gifts. I was careful and frugal with the household expenses. I bought virtually nothing for myself.

The only thing I did for myself was to steal 30,000 yen each month from the house money, put it in an envelope and send it to Sun Rise Loan and Investments. But every time I slipped the money inside the envelope and sealed it, I did it with a smile. For, thanks to Sun Rise Loan and Investments, I had finally understood the true value of my life. 30,000 yen a month seemed like a small price to pay for such contentment.

At last I understood what the priest who had married us had meant when he said that true joy comes from knowing what is important in life and getting rid of all the rest. One more thing, and this I can say for sure: not until I got into debt did I realise how much I loved my family.

A year passed in this way. And in that year I can truly say that I was a happy and satisfied woman. Then in January came the news I had been secretly praying for all winter. Haruka, my daughter, who had just turned six, had been admitted to Shirayuri, the most famous Catholic girls school in Tokyo. Haruka, being a bright child, had done well in her written exams, but so had almost all the other little girls. Again, my husband's senpai, though he had long since retired, helped. His wife was a graduate of the school and knew almost everyone on the committee.

And so, on a blustery April day, the three of us, Haruka, Ryu and I, took the metro into Shibuya and then transferred to the Hanzomon line to Kudanshita. From there we walked up the hill to the Yasukuni shrine whose giant cast-iron outer gate could be seen right from the metro exit. We joined the throngs of mothers and fathers, all of us dressed identically in our dark suits and dark dresses, the women wearing long strings of pearls. Inside the gymnasium, as the headmistress welcomed us to the school, I caught quick sideways glimpses of some of the other students and their parents and I thought of how different they looked from us. Had I made a mistake? I wondered. Would Haruka not have been happier going to a school near the house? Then I thought of myself and all that I had once dreamed of becoming. Haruka would be the world leader, or the high-powered businesswoman. Haruka would do everything I could not, I decided.

And so, every morning I woke Haruka an hour earlier than her brother and together we would take the train to Kudanshita in the heart of the city. It took us almost an hour to get there. After seeing her to the gate I would stand and wave to her from the pavement outside like the other mothers did, all of us dressed most carefully in dark dresses or skirts, a rule imposed upon us by the school.

Unlike Akira, who made no friends either in his primary or middle school, Haruka settled in quickly and made friends from the first day. Then, as Haruka grew more and more popular and it became known that she was at the top of her class, the other mothers began to look at me curiously. I kept a polite expression on my face and ignored them. We were not of the same world.

Every day, after seeing their children off, a group of mothers would go to a certain café and drink coffee together. I discovered this by chance the first day as I too was headed for a coffee before going home and, coincidentally, the café I chose was the one the other mothers came to. However, after that first day, when they entered and saw me sitting in their café at the best table by the window doing my English homework, I was careful to go to another café closer to the station. Then one day they invited me to join them for coffee. I hesitated, but seeing the refusal forming on my face, one of the mothers, the prettiest one, quickly said, "Please don't refuse. We are all dying to know more about your lovely daughter."

"But I have some homework to finish before English class," I protested weakly.

"Oh, will you be punished if you don't do it?" the same woman asked laughingly. I had to laugh. I looked at her openly for the first time and her beauty awakened memories of Tomoko. Not the adult unhappy Tomoko I had known, but another Tomoko. A married contented Tomoko. So I followed them to the coffee shop.

In the coffee shop, I was given the place of honour, right in the middle of all of them. One by one they introduced themselves. Mrs Tanabe, the one who had insisted I come, sat across from me. On either side of her were Mrs Kobayashi and Mrs Sayako Watanabe, both of whom clearly came from very good Tokyo families and who had daughters in Haruka's class. On either side of me were Mrs Okada and another Mrs Watanabe. I didn't know either of them as their children were older than Haruka. The waitress had barely taken the order and left when they began pelting me with questions.

"Your daughter is a genius in mathematics I am told," Mrs Sayako Watanabe sitting across from me said. "Did you send her to any special classes?"

I shook my head. "Special classes? I didn't know there were any for such little children."

"There certainly are. There are *Jukus* for everything these days."

"I didn't know," I said humbly. "Actually I didn't even know that my daughter was good in mathematics."

"There are special classes for everything these days," Mrs Okada said, nodding approvingly. "I never sent my girls to any either."

I felt relieved. I had passed the first test.

The Mrs Watanabe beside me said firmly, "I don't waste my time on *Jukus* but there are many things schools don't teach children these days. That is why I send my daughter to shamisen class, calligraphy class and ballet."

"Did Haruka-chan do any special classes at all?" Mrs Sayako Watanabe asked.

"Not really. I am planning to send her to piano and ballet class," I lied. The thought had not crossed my mind till that very instant. But somehow, sitting with such affluent mothers, I suddenly felt it was exactly what Haruka should do. I would find the money somehow.

"Then how did Haruka get into the school?" Mrs Kobayashi asked finally.

Now I understood why I had been invited. I took a deep breath. At that moment I was tempted to lie but something stopped me. Lies always ended up being found out. Taking a deep breath, as humbly as I could, I explained my husband's relation to his senpai's family and how much his senpai had done for us. I told it as naturally as I could and when I finished there was a short silence. Silence can be both positive and negative, but in this case it turned out to be positive. Mrs Okada was a relative of my husband's senpai's wife, and Mrs Kobayashi knew the family too. They nodded approvingly. But they hesitated to speak. I realised that Tanabe-san, the prettiest one, had still said nothing and that in fact they were all waiting for her to speak. All the time I had been speaking she had pretended to be absorbed in her coffee cup. Now she looked up, looking directly into my eyes. Her face was so serious that I felt afraid. But I refused to look away. After holding my gaze for a few seconds, looking deep into my eyes as if she were reading my soul, she smiled. It was a different kind of smile from the ones she usually gave, smaller. "Haruka-chan is a very well-brought-up girl. I hope she will have a good influence on my little Eriko," she said. In the centre of her eyes was a tiny flame of mischief.

Really beautiful people are attracted to really plain ones in just the same way that really plain ones are attracted to really beautiful ones. When Mrs Kyoko Tanabe looked into my eyes I too looked into hers and I saw there the same loneliness that I had seen in Tomoko's eyes. But in Mrs Tanabe's case, since she had a family, it was less visible. If I hadn't already seen it in Tomoko I would not have recognized it in Mrs Tanabe. But Mrs Tanabe was not Tomoko. I sensed in her a cruelty towards the world which she tried to hide under an extra careful kindness towards everyone. Which is why, at that moment, she must have decided to be kind to me. Clearly, I was not worthy of their group, but by going against her natural urge, which would have been to make fun of me and reject me, Mrs Tanabe showed how fully in control of her own nature she was.

After that, I joined them every day. It was the first time I was a part of a group. Even in school it had been only Tomoko and me. But now I was a part of eight mothers, three of them with children in Haruka's class. They were all college educated and well brought up. They had rich parents who had found them rich husbands and they all lived in apartments or houses in or around Central Tokyo, not far from where they had been born. They all possessed multiple strings of Mikimoto

122

pearls bought for them first by their parents and then by their rich, successful husbands. They wore tiny diamonds in their well-shaped ears and those that were Catholics wore a little diamond cross. They were all so pretty and well-dressed and young. I was so proud to belong to their group, so proud to walk with them in the streets and watch how the men's heads turned, so proud to sit amongst them in the café and see how the other women watched us enviously.

I was so happy, I could barely stop myself from smiling all day. And every night I looked forward to the next day—to the moment I would meet Mrs Tanabe and the others again.

Of the mothers in our group, Mrs Kobayashi was the oldest and the richest. Her second husband was twelve years her junior and it was his child from a previous marriage that she had adopted as her own. She was a very elegant lady, the most elegant lady I have ever met. She wore all black suits and carried a black crocodile skin Hermes handbag. She spoke English like a proper Englishwoman because when she was a student her parents had sent her to Oxford University in England. "Your English is very good," she complimented me one day. "I can't believe you learnt it here in Japan." Because of my good English, I think, she was always kind to me. Mrs Okada, only a little younger than Mrs Kobayashi and hardly as rich, was exactly her opposite. From the moment I joined their group, she went out of her way to make me feel like I really didn't belong. It was she who forced me to confess that I had never been to see Kabuki. I felt so humiliated then, but afterwards, when Mrs Sayako Watanabe, the quietest and least pretty of them all, invited me to join her at the Kabuki theatre in Ginza, I felt so happy I almost wanted to thank Mrs Okada for her meanness.

I didn't follow much of the play for I was far more

interested in the audience. Never had I seen such elegance! All the women wore traditional dresses—but what beautiful kimonos! I had always thought of my mother in her hostess kimonos as the most elegant woman in the world. But here were kimonos ten times as elaborate, worn with a casual grace that took my breath away. There were a few men there too and they were dressed in equally gorgeous kimonos. My eyes fell on a man and a woman sitting on one of the tatami mats at the front, the ones that cost twenty thousand per seat. The man held a fan in his hand with which he batted the air solemnly in time with the music. The woman was sitting half-facing the man so I could only see her body in profile, slender like a stalk of rice bending in the wind, the round curve of her obi emphasizing her well-shaped neck. Though she was just a silhouette, it was the woman who really held my attention. I watched her movements. She was opening an old-fashioned eight-tiered lacquer bento box and the way her hands moved were like the slow unhurried movements of a dance. I realised then that I was looking into another world, two worlds in fact, the world of the stage and the one of the audience. And that the two worlds shared something important—beauty, a beauty of gesture and time that I had never imagined existed. I looked at Mrs Watanabe sitting next to me. It was as if a light had gone on inside her, making her face briefly beautiful. She belonged to the same world too because she understood it. Just as the other mothers did. But I did not belong there. Which was why Mrs Okada was not nice to me. But then why were the others so kind? I wondered.

When I came out, I looked at the familiar buildings of Ginza and felt like I had just returned from very far away. Mrs Sayako Watanabe, the kindest lady I have ever met, asked me if I had enjoyed myself. I answered yes, absolutely. "I'm so glad," she replied sincerely. But if I try to picture her face now I cannot do so. For kindness, unlike beauty, is a taste that quickly disappears from the mind. The only one who truly remains alive in my memory is Mrs Tanabe.

*

Mrs Kyoko Tanabe was the prettiest of them all but she dressed the most plainly, in clothes that were clearly bought in the bargain sections of department stores. She hardly ever went to a hairdresser, preferring to leave her hair its natural black. She wore almost no jewellery—except two medium-sized pearls in her small perfect ears. And the make-up she used was so slight it was almost non-existent. But, I soon found out, she was married to a most successful cardiac surgeon, a genius who everyone said would one day get a Nobel prize. They lived in one of those brand-new apartment buildings in Ichibancho. Mrs Tanabe had two children, a boy and girl, named Katsuhiro and Eriko. The boy went to Gyosei school for boys and the girl Eriko was Haruka's best friend at Shirayuri. I never understood their friendship, just as I never understood Eriko's mother Mrs Tanabe. Sometimes I found myself staring at Haruka over the dining table, wishing she would tell me the secret of her power over others. For, little Eriko simply adored Haruka, worshipped her in fact. While with Kyoko, her mother, I was never sure how I would be treated. Sometimes she was very nice to me, too nice I think, so that in her niceness she made me feel small and unworthy. Other times, she was openly mean, making fun of me in front of the others, thus making the likes of Mrs Okada happy. At still other moments, she would walk me to the subway after our coffee and on the way would tell me how I was the only mother in our group who was the least bit interesting. One day, she told me I was her best friend and made me swear undying devotion to our friendship. But then the next day at coffee she ignored me so pointedly that all the others noticed. The worst part was that when I greeted her humbly each morning, I never knew how she would be with me. After a while I realised that the others were scared of her too and yet, because she was so pretty, they clung to her like moss on a rock. That was why she was lonely. And so I decided not to let her moods bother me and to remain friendly no matter what. After some time, I grew to look forward to the moment she would greet me, for not knowing what kind of greeting it would be added excitement to my life.

If you had seen me with my lady friends you would probably have found us boring. But I was happy to look boring in those days. For, being boring is the privilege of the rich. They alone don't have to worry about how they look or what others think of them. I took care to wear exactly the same dull colours and designs the others wore. And always I carried Tomoko's black Burberry with me, a silent and faithful companion. But when it came to making conversation, I was always nervous and whenever anyone asked me a direct question I felt the sweat squeeze out of my pores.

Most times the conversation started with food—how to bake the best cake, where to buy the best Western-style bread. Then it moved on to children—where to buy the best school uniform or tennis racquet, the best teacher in the school, extra classes in music—whether piano was better or violin. On these subjects, since I was a good cook and read a lot of magazines, I could contribute easily. But when talk shifted to sports or hobbies, I fell silent. All the other mothers were active members of tennis clubs and golf clubs where they went with their husbands every weekend. During the week, they did ikebana classes and studied the shamisen or koto and went to Kabuki in the afternoons. I was the only one who did not play any traditional instrument, did not belong to a tennis or golf club, had never been inside a Kabuki theatre in her life, and did not spend her weekends at the Chiba golf course.

There are moments in one's life which are like a crossroads. One takes a decision and the direction of one's life changes suddenly. But because life is like a forest, one doesn't know that one has changed directions, for the forest stretches in all directions. If only I had been busy that day, if only Haruka or Akira, Akira probably, since he was the delicate one, had fallen sick. Then I would have not have been at the school and I would not have said yes to the lunch. Not till much, much later did I realise the price of that one word spoken with such joy and anticipation in my heart.

The restaurant was called Enchantement and it was French, but the cook was Japanese. Lately, Kateigaho, the very expensive magazine they all read, had done a big article on French food in Tokyo cooked by Japanese chefs. Enchantement had been highlighted because the chef had won a prize in France the previous summer. Because it was so popular, reservations were hard to get and people had to book months in advance. But Mrs Okada, who was terribly well-connected had managed to get us a table for four because she and her husband played golf with the owner of the restaurant building. I was there when the restaurant had first been mentioned and I was also there when Mrs Okada, her eyes sparkling, told us of her "connection" to the restaurant and how she had managed to get a table for the end of May. Since she didn't like me, I never paid much attention to Mrs Okada. I didn't dream I would be invited to join them. As you can imagine, I was very surprised. I could not understand why I had been chosen. "But please don't say anything to the others," Mrs Tanabe warned me, letting it be understood that I had been given a privilege. "You understand I had to fight hard for you. I persuaded Mrs Okada by telling her she could choose the other person freely." Immediately my mind began to ask who the fourth woman might be. I hoped that it would be the kind Mrs Sayako Watanabe. But then my mind answered that it would probably be Mrs Kobayashi for she was the sister-in-law of the emperor's aunt's grandnephew and of course she was very rich too. "Thank you so much. I am indebted to you," I replied humbly.

"*Tondemo nai*," Mrs Tanabe said, looking pleased, it was nothing. "I tell you what," she added, "if you like, we can ask the same kimono lady to tie both our kimonos. I know the perfect woman, she is a neighbour, and she knows how to dress the hair as well." She grabbed my arm in her excitement, "Oh please say yes, it will be such fun to get dressed together."

How could I refuse? Even a strong person could not have refused such a request.

The reservation was for 29 May, so we had a little less than seven weeks to wait. But from the moment Tanabe Kyoko invited me, I could think of little else. What did the inside of a chic French restaurant look like? I wondered. What would the other people be wearing? I had never tasted French cuisine. Would I like it? I imagined a large white room like a ballroom with French windows and a crystal chandelier. I saw our table decorated with white roses. I dreamed that we would all have a wonderful time and become the best of friends.

Then, one morning, when my eyes opened, a new and terrible thought presented itself. I didn't have a kimono. Not even one.

Normally, a Japanese girl inherits several carefully preserved kimonos from her mother, receives a splendid new one for her twentieth year coming-out day and another for marriage. Then, over the years, she acquires a few more which she eventually passes on to her daughter. But my mother had given me none because she mostly owned geisha kimonos which she used at work. As for my marriage, since she had wanted no part of it, I had rented a kimono. I thought longingly of the 1.5 million she had given me that one time she visited me: why had I not held on to it or given it to my husband instead of spending it uselessly on designer leftovers? I thought briefly of renting a kimono again but quickly gave up the idea. Rented kimonos were immediately noticeable for their smell—and of course, by the little red tag on the inside hem giving the name and telephone number of the rental company. In my mind I saw the faces of my friends as they digested the fact that I had come to lunch in a rented kimono. Then I remembered that I had promised to dress with Mrs Tanabe and that the kimono and the hairdresser would cost 25,000 yen. I closed my eyes and groaned. I thought briefly about borrowing one from my neighbour, the obaa-chan who sometimes baby-sat for us, but quickly dismissed the idea for I knew that nothing she had would be grand enough for my lunch. And what about a new kimono, a tiny voice whispered. I turned towards Ryu, who was still fast asleep beside me and poked him hard. "Ryu, wake up. I have to buy a kimono," I told him.

It took him a few minutes to come into full consciousness. "A kimono? Is someone we know getting married?" he asked.

"No. But I don't have a single kimono. What kind of Japanese woman has no kimono of her own? If I have to go for a formal event somewhere, what will I do?"

"You don't need to worry. We are with an American company now. No need for kimono."

"But still, what about when I go out with friends?" I cried, knowing I was losing.

"Wear something else," Ryu muttered, settling down for another hour's sleep.

Ryu didn't forget about my kimono. The following day, when we arrived at his mother's house in Kyushu he asked her if she could spare a kimono for me. "Our Kayo needs a kimono to go out with her conservative new friends."

His mother looked surprised. "Didn't her mother give her any?"

Right from the first day of our marriage they talked about me as if I wasn't in the same room as them. At first it had made me very angry but now I was so used to it I didn't notice. "All my mother's kimonos were burnt in a fire," I lied.

The day we left, my mother-in-law gave me a carefully wrapped parcel and for a while, until I opened it and saw the stains, I was truly grateful to her.

In this way, the holidays passed and school began again. Now there were only three weeks left till the dreaded lunch. As I was walking up to the school, Kyoko Tanabe grabbed me. "I have a special favour to ask of you," she said. "Will you come with me to buy a new kimono on Thursday? All my kimonos are so old-fashioned and out of date. And you have such good taste."

The word "kimono" sent a shiver through me. Had Kyoko read my mind? Did she know that I had no kimono? Was she doing this to taunt me? Seeing me hesitate, she doubled her entreaties. "Oh please say yes, Kayo-san, you are the only friend I have. I really, really want to go with you."

I could not say no.

In the coffee shop, Mrs Watanabe, the kind one, whispered into my ear, "I hear you will be going to the French restaurant with Tanabe-san and Okada-san. I am so happy for you."

Tears came to my eyes. Mrs Watanabe saw them and concern flooded her face. "You deserve it, you really do," she said.

For a second I was tempted to ask her to lend me a kimono. But then I imagined the look on her face and banished the idea.

On Tuesday and Wednesday I pretended to have my monthly sickness and made my husband take Haruka to school. I really did feel sick, but it was a sickness of the spirit. All day I stayed inside the house and cleaned till I was so tired I could not move a finger. Then on Wednesday afternoon I received a call from Tanabe-san. "Are you all right, Kayo-san?" she asked, using my given name. I was so surprised I couldn't think of what to say. It was the first time anyone from the group had called me at home.

"I was feeling a little unwell but I am better now," I lied. "It must have been the holidays."

"Holidays are tiring, aren't they?" she agreed. "So will you be coming to school tomorrow then?"

"I suppose so," I replied, my heart heavy.

"Wonderful, then we can go to Ginza right after our coffee. The department stores all open at ten."

"Of course," I replied.

"What about your English class though?" she asked.

"English?" I had forgotten about the class. In order to save a little money I had stopped the class a short while after joining the group. "I can miss one class. Don't worry," I said.

"Thank you so much. *Mata ne,*" she said and hung up.

When the house was silent again, I thought to myself that maybe the gods were giving me an opportunity to tell Tanabe-san that I wasn't going to be able to come for the lunch.

Another strange thing happened. The same afternoon, I found a thick letter addressed to me in the mailbox. I opened it and inside was a new credit card from the bank. I looked at it in disgust. Why were they sending me a card when I had already told them a year earlier that I didn't want it? I decided I would go to the bank after buying the kimono and return the card in person.

The next day, my eyes opened at 4.30 a.m. despite falling asleep well after midnight. I had a heavy feeling in my heart. I didn't want to go out. Staring up at the low white ceiling of our room, the thought came to me that the house was my shell and I was a just-born bird. How could I survive outside my shell? But time moves on relentlessly and soon I heard the birds calling and bright spring sunlight slipped through the chinks in the curtains. But the heavy feeling in my heart stayed with me till I got out of the metro at Kudanshita. Only when I saw the iron gate of Yasukuni shrine in front of me and the Budokan and Chidorigafuchi to the left did it vanish and my heart grew light and whole again. It was as if my two days in the house had left my spirit drained and empty and now the familiar sights and sounds of the big city were slowly filling it up again. By the time I met the other mothers and we began our daily pilgrimage to the coffee shop I was feeling quite different. I had missed the city, I realised.

After the other mothers left one by one, Mrs Tanabe and I lingered in the coffee shop. We ordered a round of freshly squeezed orange juice, something they had just introduced after the holidays.

"To give us strength for shopping," Mrs Tanabe said, winking at me.

I felt both nervous and excited. Mrs Tanabe was looking exceptionally beautiful that day. Her navy suit was of an expensive fabric and so well cut it had to be Italian. She was wearing a thick double string of pearls. Her hair was loose and framing her heart-shaped face, and she'd obviously taken great care with her make-up. Against the dark wooden background of the booth she seemed to glow like a firefly, I thought.

Then I glanced at my own reflection in the window; I wasn't looking too bad either I thought. On the other side of the window, the last of the hordes of salaried men were coming into work and many glanced at the two of us with desire in their eyes. All of a sudden, I felt excited to be going shopping with Kyoko Tanabe.

The feeling was so strong, it was like lightning shooting through my body.

We paid our bill and left. On the way to the metro, Kyoko-san was in a good mood and chattered gaily about French cuisine in France, her week at her in-laws' country house in Karuizawa, the weather. I felt like I was in the company of an exotic bird. We took the Yurakucho line and got off at Ginza-Itchome, right opposite Matsuya. Memories came flooding back, of my first meeting with Tomoko especially. At the corner of Chanel, we turned down a side street and arrived at the quiet Ginza Nichome. Here, the past still clung to the street. The shops were smaller and the displays were simpler. And they were interspersed with old- fashioned soba restaurants. But Kyoko-san led me confidently down the street.

"Where are we going?" I asked.

She stopped and turned. "You mean you don't know Ginza Echigoya?"

"Oh that shop, I didn't know it still existed," I lied.

"Where do you go for your kimonos?" she asked.

"Me? Oh I prefer Matsuya," I lied again.

"Matsuya? They have kimonos?" She glanced in the direction of the giant department store and her step faltered. "But Echigoya is the oldest and most famous shop in Ginza. My husband's family has always gone there." And with that she turned her back to me and continued walking down the street. I followed her, feeling satisfied. I had succeeded in making her doubt herself. Now she thought that I knew something she didn't. We passed an art gallery, Aoyama Yofuku—a cheap western clothing store, a bookstore, a hat shop and then we arrived at Echigoya.

It was a very modest-looking entrance for such a famous shop—an old-fashioned glass door with one of those handles that you grabbed and pushed down to make the door open, not even an automatic door, a small display window with four narrow bands of cloth, two of them kimono fabrics and two obis. Kyoko was already talking to the salesman at the counter at the back of the store when I entered. I glanced around me curiously but was even more disappointed by the interior of the shop. On the left-hand wall were three more kimono and obi materials sets. One was in grey, the other in beige and the third in purple. What boring colours, I thought. In an old-fashioned glass case in the middle of the room were several obi rolls. And on the other side of the shop, against the wall, was an old kimono, nothing particularly special about it, except that it was white in colour and obviously old.

"That kimono was made by us for the Showa Empress," a voice said just behind me. I turned quickly. I had not noticed the second man enter quietly from the back room. He was dressed conservatively in a black suit and a maroon necktie. But from the way he spoke I could tell I was talking to the owner or the son of the owner of the shop. I was impressed, both by him and by what he had just told me.

"Are you looking for spring kimono or something else?" he asked.

I shook my head and was about to tell him that I was only here to accompany my friend when Tanabe-san, turning to ask me for an opinion, heard the question and replied for me, "Of course she wants a new kimono." Then, coming over to me, she greeted the owner (for it was indeed the owner) and introduced me. They spoke for a few minutes, the owner asking after Tanabe-san's family and her parents-in-law. Then he turned to me again, his manner even more polite and respectful. "May I show you some of my new kimono designs? I am afraid I don't have as much as I used to have for pretty young ladies. Most of my clients are older women. But I think I may have a few special pieces that might please you."

I could not say anything. No-one had ever talked to me so politely. With little mincing steps he went behind the counter to the giant cupboard lining the back of the shop and opened the sliding doors to reveal thousands of rolls of cloth. Quickly, efficiently, he pulled out four or five. But before he could open them for me, Tanabe-san created a diversion by asking us what we thought of her choice, a dull brown cloth, with a design of splendid blue hydrangea flowers, their petals blown by the wind. The obi she chose was a brocade piece in dull gold shot through with silver and blue. She pirouetted once and then twice, the second time a little faster.

"What do you think?"

"On you everything looks wonderful," the owner of the shop replied.

"And you?" Kyoko turned to me. "What do you think?"

"I think it is nice, but..." I stopped, trying to find words that would not offend her.

"But what?" she demanded impatiently, a tiny frown appearing between her eyes.

"It's just that the colours are a little old. Don't you want a brighter colour perhaps?"

"But because madam is young, the colours look young on

her," the salesman said quickly.

We all turned to the owner who was looking thoughtful and waited for him to give his opinion.

He massaged his small pudgy chin and then replied, glancing at me, "Madame has a very fine eye. The obi is what makes the dress look old. We need a brighter, younger obi, I think I know exactly which one will be perfect." And he danced around to the glass case with the obis and opened a drawer.

"Here," he said, turning to us triumphantly. The obi was a splendid gold and silver in traditional wave pattern. He held it against the brown fabric and it came alive, the extreme traditional pattern of the obi contrasting nicely with the rather modern colours and design of the kimono fabric. Kyoko looked at it critically. "I don't know, it seems a little bright to me."

"Not at all," I said quickly, "it brings the kimono alive." I truly meant it. The obi worked like magic, transforming the dull brown kimono material into something unusual, worth looking closely at.

"Earth and water. There is balance now," the owner stated.

Kyoko looked at the price and gave a little shriek. "398,000! I cannot buy that."

"Don't worry about the price," the owner said quickly, "it is so perfect on your kimono that I will give you a thirty per cent discount."

My friend bit her lip and pretended to look indecisive.

"Take it," I urged. "Otherwise you will regret it." We waited tensely for her answer. At last she nodded and we all began to congratulate her at the same time. After the salesman had taken her into the back room for measurements, the shop owner turned to me. For a long minute he said nothing and I grew embarrassed waiting. Then he said, "You have a perfect figure for a kimono."

I was surprised. Out of the corner of my eyes I looked doubtfully at my profile in the mirror. Did I really have the perfect figure for a kimono?

"You don't believe me? Here, let me show you." He came up to me with a roll of blue cloth and deftly swung it over my left shoulder. Then he did the same on the right shoulder. The cloth flowed like water to my feet and the same design of waves appeared. But the waves on the kimono were nothing like the waves on the obi. These ones were embroidered in white, grey and gold, and they leapt out aggressively like young stallions. I gasped. The cloth seemed alive. The owner brought over a scarlet-coloured obi and placed it against the deep blue cloth.

"Here you are, a unique design—for a uniquely beautiful woman."

I stared at my reflection in the mirror. The red of the obi made the blue of the kimono glow like deep sea water. The dark blue silk emphasized the shape of my breasts, at the same time making them look more elegant and not so big. Lower down, the wave burst out of the cloth like sea horses eager to reach the shore. I lifted my arms and the motion made the waves on the sleeves dance. How can I put into words what I felt then? It was a feeling I had never had and have never had since. It was like coming home. But the home I came to was a home I had never known, a home inside my own skin. The silk fell over my arms familiarly, making them appear longer and more graceful. Suddenly I remembered the couple I had seen in the Kabuki theatre in Ginza, seeing again the grace of the woman's arms as she opened the bento for her man. I felt that grace enter my own arms as slowly I brought them down to rest on either side of my body. "This dress was made for you," the owner of Echigoya said softly, coming up behind me. In the mirror my eyes met his and I could see that he was speaking the truth.

In the end it was all surprisingly easy. I took out the credit card from my bag and gave it to the salesman. I signed the little blue slip of paper with 787,000 yen written on it. Then everyone congratulated me as if I had won the lottery and indeed I felt as if I had. Kyoko-san made them promise to give it to us in less than three weeks and she even offered to pick mine up when she came to pick up her own and to keep it with her till the day of the luncheon party.

The lunch? What can I tell you about it? I remember little of the restaurant and almost nothing of the food. I cannot tell you the name of a single thing I ate that day. All I remember was the weight of the brand-new debt on my shoulders and the heavy scent of hair lacquer in my highly decorated hair. I remember what the other ladies were wearing though. Mrs Okada had on a silver kimono with a decoration of fans across the front. Her maroon obi was entirely brocade and had a most complex geometrical pattern. She had an exquisite ruby and pearl brooch pinned on the obi. Mrs Kobayashi was wearing a pale pistachio-coloured kimono with a flying crane pattern and a golden brocade obi. They were already seated when we arrived but stood up to greet us in such accents of delight that you would have thought we were meeting after a year. The room was filled with women and I was conscious of their eyes on my kimono. But their glances gave me no pleasure. (There was one man in the room but he was sitting alone in a corner, his face buried in a book, and so I only noticed him later.) A very elegant maitre d'hotel in black and white came up to us and handed out menus the way teachers hand out exam papers. I looked at the price on the bottom and reached for the glass of iced water in front of me.

"Shall we order wine?" Mrs Okada said.

"Of course, I love wine," Kyoko agreed. "Last year my husband took me with him for a conference in Austria and we drank lots of it because it was so cheap there."

"So shall I order white then?" Mrs Okada continued.

"I prefer red," Tanabe-san said.

"Red wine is heavy. Besides, in Austria they drink white wine," Mrs Okada answered a little stiffly.

"Why don't we get both?" suggested Mrs Kobayashi, playing the role of peacemaker.

"That will be too much, we will get drunk," I said hastily, thinking of the bill.

"Let's order by the glass, then we can have both," suggested Mrs Kobayashi. In the end we ordered a bottle of white wine to please Mrs Okada and a glass of red wine each for the meat course. With each course, first Mrs Okada, then Kyoko, then Mrs Kobayashi told a story of some other fantastic meal they had enjoyed at an expensive ryokan or at a Michelin starred restaurant in Europe, describing each course in loving detail. I looked at my friend in surprise. Kyoko-san seemed to have travelled all over, but she preferred Germany and Austria. Mrs Okada went twice a year to France. Mrs Kobayashi preferred ryokans in Izu. When it came to my turn I modestly described a French cooking class I had taken and how shocked I had been by the amount of butter and cream we'd used. Everyone laughed, feeling comfortably superior, and from there the conversation turned quite naturally to the old, old topic of health and weight problems. My mind wandered, replaying the scene in the kimono shop and trying out alternative scenarios in which I had managed to say no.

I think of that lunch now as a farewell lunch. Everyone was kind to me. Mrs Kobayashi praised my beautiful new kimono and hair. Mrs Okada said she was glad I had been able to join them. Kyoko told everyone about how much fun we had had getting dressed together, making it clear to all of them that I was her special friend. The others listened and were impressed and they complimented both of us again on our kimonos and hair. The food came, elegantly arranged on the plate and in tiny ladylike portions. Everything was perfect. And yet I can remember nothing of it, for the person sitting at that table was already a ghost. One detail I can recall perfectly. I paid for the lunch with my husband's credit card, and though the bill came to 15,000 yen per person, he said nothing to me about it.

After that I never took Haruka to school again. We still went together till Kudanshita. But there, at the mouth of the station, I would stop and let her go on alone. At first she cried and made a fuss. Then she walked off without a single backward glance. I stood at the exit of the metro and watched her till her small determined back passed through the iron torii of the Yasukuni shrine.

Lotus in a Pond of Lotuses

Whenever I think of money, I see a pond full of lotuses. The lotuses are knee deep in mud, but still they are incredibly beautiful. What a miracle! A miracle made by nature. Though the lotus is born in the mud, is nourished by the mud and dies in it, the lotus remains the most pure thing a person can imagine. For the lotus rises up above the mud so perfect in form and colour that no-one looking at it remembers what lies at its feet. That is why in Buddhism we worship the lotus. Money is the same. Like the lotus, no matter where it comes from, or in whose hands it is, money is money, it doesn't change. It doesn't show where it has been or what has been done to obtain it. It looks always the same and the sight of it makes a person happy.

I had never desired money. Not even when I was young. In reality few Japanese do. That is why we are not really good at business. For a Japanese, money cannot ever be a goal in itself. But, for some of us, there comes a time when money becomes a goal in itself. When a person realises that he or she will do anything for money, that person is on their way to becoming like the lotus—pure and exquisitely beautiful on top but their feet planted firmly in mud.

With the purchase of the kimono I became indebted to the bank and to Sun Rise Loan and Investments. The kimono had cost 787,000 yen. By the time I bought all the accessories and paid for the tailoring charges, the total came to almost 1,000,000 yen.

There was nothing for me to do but return to Sun Rise Loan and Investments and ask them for another loan to pay off the bank.

The mind plays such tricks. When I had gone to Sun Rise Loan and Investments the first time, I had sworn to myself never to return to that horrible office. Now I looked forward to seeing the terrible Mr Yamashita again. Even the thought of him brought me a measure of relief, for I trusted the yakuza not to betray me. Yakuza, being human, understood humans and knew how to treat them. The bank I was not so sure about. Banks had their rules, and account books were their gods. I even drew a strange kind of comfort from the fact that my father too, when his debts grew too big from him, had chosen the yakuza over the banks.

It was raining the second time I visited. The same woman opened the door and ushered me in. She seemed not to recognize me. I was made to wait in the same seat in which I had sat the previous time. Mr Yamashita was once again on the phone. This time he did not cut his call short on seeing me. He looked angry and was frowning as he stared out of the window at the rain. Inside the room, it was warm and humid. The window-pane was all fogged up because of the humidity and the raindrops made little rivers of light on its surface. So absorbed was I in watching them that I didn't notice that Mr Yamashita had gotten off the phone and was staring at me.

"Why have you come here, how did you get this address?" he asked roughly.

"I... don't you remember, I came here for a loan a little over a year ago, Mr Yamashita. Mr Maruyama of Shinsei bank sent me?" I stammered.

His face cleared, his eyes travelled to my breasts and he smiled. "Ah yes, Mr Marugame. Of course. How is he?"

"I have no idea. I don't keep in touch with the bank."

"I see." He waited for me to continue.

"I have come to you because I need another loan," I said bluntly. With Mr Yamashita I knew I didn't have to be polite.

"Another loan? Have you been overspending again?"

"I couldn't help it," I said.

"Don't tell me your child was sick, I've heard that too many times."

My head shot up. "I need a million," I blurted out.

"One million! Last time it was only 500,000. What is your husband doing treating you so badly?"

"It has got nothing to do with my husband," I said stiffly. "This is all my fault and I will pay it back. And it was 400,000 last time, not 500,000," I corrected him.

To my surprise, he laughed. "I like you, Mrs Nakayama, or whoever you are. I like you because though you won't tell me your name I can see that you have honour. So I will give you your loan, even though normally I never give the same person a second loan before that person has paid the first off. But in your case I will make an exception. Do you know why?" He leaned over the desk, his face just inches from mine. "Because I trust you. Which means I expect you not to betray me."

I nodded, unable to look away.

And so once again, I walked away from Sun Rise Loan and Investments with money in my purse. It was not much, only twenty eight thousand, as the rest was being sent directly to the bank. But it felt good. I felt light and carefree again. As I was walking down the main avenue to Gotanda station, a lace jacket caught my eye. It was displayed in the window of a small shop, you know, one of the many millions of tiny shops run by single women living in their parents' homes, and filled with all kinds of junk. But this jacket was different from the rest. It stood out. It was elegant and white and European looking. I looked at it and knew it would look just perfect with any number of my clothes. I thought, I have time, the children don't get home for another hour, let me just go in and try it on, just to see if I am right. Of course I wasn't planning to buy it.

The moment I entered the shop, the salesgirl (who wasn't, as I had imagined, an aging spinster but a fashionable Shibuya girl in shorts, false eyelashes and long carefully curled light brown hair) greeted me like a long-lost friend and gave me the jacket and a pretty yellow dress with white flowers printed all over to try on with it. She was very good at her job, for the dress and the jacket really did look wonderful together. I stared at my reflection in the mirror, unable to recognize myself. Just minutes before, I had looked like a boring housewife and now I looked like a young girl again. Just then the salesgirl knocked and asked if she could see. So I opened the curtain and went into the shop.

"*Subarashi!*" she exclaimed. "I would not have recognized you. To be honest, when you went inside I had second thoughts. I thought I had made a mistake with the dress, that it would be a bit too young for you. But now I see that my instinct was right. They look perfect on you."

I looked at myself through her eyes. It is a strange thing—when a beautiful woman tells an ordinary one that something looks good on her the latter always believes her. Even when the beautiful one is clearly lying, the ordinary one believes her. This is because she has fallen under beauty's spell. Confusing beauty with goodness, the ordinary woman believes the beautiful one. There and then I threw away all the excuses of why I wouldn't buy, and began to wonder how I could buy them both, the jacket and the yellow dress.

The scent of new clothes, to one who has not smelt it in a long time, is like alcohol to an alcoholic. It fills the brain with bubbles of joy, clouds reason, makes the impossible seem possible. My husband always said how careful one had to be when one went out with clients. "Caution melts inside a glass of alcohol," he'd say, "you have no idea the number of bad loans that have been made because of it."

My alcohol was and is the scent of new clothes. That day, it was a scent I had not experienced since I got into debt the first time. And so I was powerless against its effect. I bought the dress and jacket, putting a little onto Ryu's card, and paying for the rest with the loan money and the household money.

That night's dinner put everyone in a bad mood. Haruka was the most vocal about it. "Rice and vegetables? Is that all you can give us? How am I supposed to study on rice and vegetables?"

But surprisingly, Ryu defended me. "Don't talk to your mother like that!" he said sharply.

Haruka looked shocked, for she was Ryu's favourite.

"Vegetables are good for your health. Only Americans eat meat every day. And look what happens to their bodies. Fat and bloated like giant radishes..."

"Yes, look at them," Haruka shot back, "they are bigger and stronger than us. That is why they beat us in the war."

"Tomorrow you will have steak, okay?" I said, feeling terrible. Haruka gave me a grateful smile.

That night, Ryu said something that surprised me. "You look happy today," he said. I was sitting in front of the mirror, brushing my hair and thinking of my beautiful yellow dress and the white jacket still in its cellophane wrapping.

I started guiltily at the sound of his voice. "Who were you

thinking of?" he asked. I should have said that I was thinking of him but he would have known it was a lie. We had been married too long.

I shrugged. "Nobody."

To my surprise, the happy feeling stayed with me for almost a week. Each time I saw the yellow dress hanging in my cupboard I felt as if a window to a wonderful new world had opened for me and I had only to put the dress on for that world to be mine. My debts and the terrible food I was giving my husband and children day after day—none of that had any power over me. But eventually the scent of newness faded away and was replaced by a very familiar old smell, something slightly stale, like old cabbage and onions. After that I wore the yellow and white dress less and less because each time I wore it I found some new blemish in myself. Soon I started disliking the jacket and dress so much that I sold them to a second-hand clothing store in Shinjuku for two thousand. The jacket and dress had cost me close to fifty thousand. But the thought of the nice empty gap in my wardrobe made me happy. I promised myself I would not do it again.

But then, a few days later, while walking out of Kichijoji station, I saw another dress, a chic black cocktail thing that was deceptively simple and yet terribly elegant. It wasn't a designer dress but somehow it had the look and feel of one. Once more, the lovely feeling of wanting something blindly blossomed inside me. It is a feeling better than love, that feeling. Maybe it is love, I don't really know. I couldn't help myself. The price was more than I could afford but I had to have it. So again I used Ryu's credit card and some of the house money to do so. At the time I didn't feel guilty or even think about it, I just knew I had to have the dress and there was no room for any other thought in my head. I felt so happy that

I had seen the dress and could buy it before anyone else got it. I was the harbour. The dress was the lost boat. I was just so relieved we had found each other.

Some days later, at the hairdressers', I came upon an article in a magazine. It claimed that the best way to remain young was to feel happy inside. The article, written by an American doctor and translated into Japanese by a well-known woman writer, suggested that even if she were young, a woman should do one thing a day that gave her pleasure, whether it was a hobby, sports, yoga or food, for that way she would be able to prolong her youth.

Normally, such an article would not have interested me at all but as I was about to turn to another page I looked up and saw my face in the mirror. In the unforgiving neon light of the beauty parlour, with my hair in curlers and wrapped in a plastic cloth and almost no make-up on my face, I saw each and every change that was about to happen to my face. Age, I saw, was already biting into my cheeks, my neck and my forehead and feasting on my youth. I tried to look away and noticed someone else in the mirror, another client, sitting diagonally behind me. She was old, and her wrinkled face was utterly beyond saving. But she was smiling flirtatiously at the pretty young man drying her hair. I felt shocked. What was such an old woman doing in a beauty parlour? Why didn't she just hide herself away? At the same time, a thought struck me that all the women in the parlour with me were no longer really beautiful anyway. Then I looked at myself again, really looked I mean. I saw that my eyes were no longer so bright and the skin on my neck had three fine lines. Two lines had begun to appear around my mouth just in the crease of my nose and beside my lips.

That day I knew that I had finally seen the face of my

enemy. And my life changed. I became a warrior. I was going to fight age, I decided. I was going to be happy at any cost because being happy was the only way to remain young. Life-changing moments are not supposed to come inside a beauty parlour while reading a magazine. But that is how life is. It surprises you, taking you in directions you would not dream of. That is how it was with me. After that day, I decided never to live without shopping again. For the pleasure it gave me was better than any hobby, sport or food. And because the pleasure lasted longer than a few hours, it was less expensive than a sports club or a hobby or going to restaurants.

Having decided this, my next big problem was money. Ryu had never forbidden me to use his bank's credit card but I didn't want to use it. So I decided to get a part-time job and make my own money. Since the children only came back from school at seven in the evening most weekdays, I had lots of spare time. I didn't care what I did but I thought that I would be good at selling. I dressed well and talked well and knew what women liked. So I went to the big department stores, filled out a long application form in triplicate, attached a photo, and then waited for an answer. Eventually, the answer came. It was short and to the point and the signature was printed not signed. "Thank you for your interest in working with us but right now there is no job for a person with your qualifications." Then I tried the smart cafés around Jiyugaoka and Den-en-Chofu. But the problem there was that I had no work experience, and they all wanted people who had already worked in café's. Finally, I tried the doctors' and dentists' offices, but no-one wanted someone part-time, everyone wanted somebody young and full-time.

One day, as I returned from yet another fruitless job hunt, I passed as usual the Pink Pelican pachinko parlour with its fake palm trees on either side of the entrance. But this time, instead of crossing the road or looking away, I looked directly at the entrance of the building and paused. Two men were smoking cigarettes at the entrance. They could not have been more different. One was a young punk with steel chains everywhere and long, strangely cut hair with a purple highlight. The other was in his late sixties, with thinning grey hair and a worrier's face. They both looked at me as I walked past them and so I straightened my back immediately and stuck my chest out just a little. I went straight up to the office on the second floor and entered without knocking.

After the noise of the machines, each blaring out its mindless tune at a different rhythm and tempo, the silence inside the office was deafening. The same discreet goldfish swam in lazy aimless circles in the aquarium. The same black leather sofas where I had sat now waited for someone to fill them. And the same closed circuit black and white TVs showed the unlucky and the lucky at play. The room was occupied by three people—the two Korean girls I already knew, and a man. The man was badly dressed and short, the kind of man you would never notice even if he was standing right in front of you. I concentrated exclusively on the girls. At first they didn't remember me.

"Hello. Do you remember me?" I said confidently.

They looked at each other nervously. "I was almost run over by your boss and you gave me tea in this very room afterwards and let me play."

Then, turning to the second girl, I added, "It was the end of winter and you were admiring my black Burberry coat."

Their faces cleared and they gave me their professional smiles. "I remember, you were very lucky, you won," the shorter one said.

"Yes," I said, looking hard at them, "generally I am quite lucky. I am looking for a job. Do you think you can help me?"

The girls looked at me blankly. Their eyes slid nervously to the right, in the direction of the man.

"Remember you said I dressed nicely and would pull in many customers. What do you think about my working with you?" I said desperately, taking a step closer.

Silence. The goldfish began to dart back and forth, opening and closing their mouths in alarm.

The taller one came to life suddenly and, stepping towards me, said, "Look, that is very kind of you to offer to work here but you know it is very noisy here and may be too much for your nerves."

"My nerves are strong," I replied.

"But we are not looking for anyone right now. If you want to go down and play, I can show you a free machine," she replied. The shorter one stepped forward as well, forming a human wall in front of me.

Suddenly my courage deserted me. I took a step back, my body shrinking in defeat.

"Just one moment." The man who had been sitting silently and watching us all this time suddenly got up and stepped around the desk. I turned to him like a flower looking for sunlight. He had such a nice, calm, kind voice. "What kind of work are you looking for?"

"Anything," I replied. "I will do anything. But I can only do it part-time."

The girls laughed nervously, and the short one, who now made no secret of the fact that she wanted to get rid of me, said, "Then there is nothing for you here. We take people full-time only."

The other girl laughed nervously and nodded in agreement.

"Wait a minute, be quiet," the man ordered. "I am in charge here."

Obediently the two stepped back, heads lowered.

"Go downstairs and make yourselves useful," he ordered, "and bring this lady some tea."

And that is how I came to do the job I am now doing. After the girls had left, the man apologised for their rudeness and invited me to sit down on the sofa.

"You know you are lucky I was here today. There are not so many jobs in Japan any more, especially no part-time ones. Too many young people looking for jobs after the crisis you see." He took out a card and offered it to me. "Let me introduce myself, I am Mr Park. I am the general manager of Pelican group."

He was so polite that I was almost convinced he was Japanese and had simply chosen a Korean name. He must be Korean-Japanese, I thought.

"Pleased to meet you," I murmured shyly. "Do you think you might have something for me then?"

"Depends on what kind of work you are looking for," he answered. Then, leaning close to me, he said, "Do you mind if I ask you a question? Why are you looking to work?"

I looked at him in panic. No-one had asked me this question before.

"You should tell me the truth," he said gently. "I have a talent. I can always smell a lie."

So I told him the truth but as little as possible, "I have a debt," I replied.

"To the bank?"

"Yes," I lied, but he didn't seem to notice.

"You want to pay it off before your husband notices."

I nodded.

"That is good." The first time. Of course you would want to know about the first time. But in this kind of job, before the first time there is an audition.

"Take off your shirt," Mr Park said. I was so shocked I couldn't move. "Take off your shirt. I want to see your breasts," he said again. Taking that shirt off was the most difficult thing I ever did. Do you want to know how I did it? I imagined I was in high school again and I was taking off my shirt in front of Ryu. It wasn't so difficult then, for Mr Park was small and thin just like Ryu.

When Mr Park saw my breasts I could tell he was impressed. I looked down at them, at their huge swelling whiteness and felt distinctly proud. Then I thought of the clothes I would buy, and I didn't think of anything else till Mr Park told me I could put my bra and my shirt back on.

"Though you aren't young any more, so we will have to put your price quite low to start with, you will have no trouble getting customers with those big beauties of yours. Soon you will be making so much money you won't know how to spend it all," he said as he walked me out and down the stairs at the entrance of the Pink Pelican pachinko parlour. "I will call you and fix a time that is convenient. Just remember to send me the fifty per cent every month. And don't try to cheat, because we keep careful accounts."

"I won't," I replied uncertainly.

Mr Park didn't call for a week. I began to think he had forgotten about me. The feeling of his cold fish-like hands on my breasts began to fade and I began to think I had had a lucky escape. I would pay off my debt slowly, I decided. I would never buy a new dress again. I would be an obedient wife and a good mother.

Then one day the telephone rang. It was Mr Park. "This

is Park," he said briefly. "You still want to do it?" The feeling of Mr Park's hands on my breasts returned, as fresh as if it had happened yesterday. I hesitated. How many more hands would put their mark on me if I said yes? I almost told him that I wouldn't but then I pictured myself walking into a shop with money to spend and my desire nearly consumed me. When I still didn't reply, Mr Park grew impatient. "Listen, you came to me begging for a job, you want to do it or not? I am a busy man..."

"Y-yes," I replied quickly. "Yes, I will."

Mr Park's words cut off in midstream. Then, in a voice quite different from the businesslike one he'd used before, he said, "Good girl. I knew you'd see sense. Listen, I have got you a really great client, One of our best customers, in fact. Young, good-looking, tall. A real *shyacho*, not some stupid salaried man who only gets pocket money from his wife, you know what I mean?"

As he was talking, my mind had flown to Tokyo—to Ginza, to Marounouchi, to Omotesando Dori. I imagined myself walking down those streets, elegant and carefree, my hand on the arm of a handsome businessman.

"Hey, why so quiet? Don't you want money? You are going to be rich," Mr Park said, suddenly breaking into heavily accented English.

"*Unh*," I agreed, seeing Tomoko as I had first seen her, resplendent in her murasaki-coloured Chanel suit. His voice warmly seductive, Mr Park continued. "He is from Kita-Kyushu and comes to Tokyo once or twice a month. Dress really elegant, he wants an expensive Tokyo woman."

"And I am an expensive Tokyo woman?" I asked doubtfully.

"Now you are," he replied.

A few hours later he called again. "It's all fixed up. Meet

me at Shibuya by the Hachiko statue on Thursday at 2.30 p.m." When I arrived at the meeting place it was crowded with young people and I felt like an alien from outer space. I looked at their silly clothes and outrageous expensive hairstyles and felt angry. Did they even think of their mothers and wonder what those poor women were doing in their boxy homes? Did they think of anyone except themselves? Then a new thought struck me: what if my son was one of them? What if he was here too and was looking at me right now? I was about to turn and go back inside the station when Mr Park found me. I greeted him with fake enthusiasm and he gave my arm a reassuring squeeze. "Don't worry," he whispered, "everything will be fine." They were stupid words but somehow, coming from his mouth, I believed them.

Still holding my arm, Mr Park guided me confidently through the maze of Dogenzaka streets and stopped before a blue and white stucco building of four floors. The love hotel was called Au Clair de Lune which I later learnt means moonlight in French. Though it was a sunny day, the strange thing about Dogenzaka is that no sunlight ever penetrates. So, day is only a weaker, greyer version of the night and all love hotels keep their neon signs on twenty-four hours of the day.

Mr Park let go of my arm. "Go to the reception and ask for the key to room 504. Then go to the room. He is waiting for you."

All my doubts returned. I looked at him fearfully, my eyes begging silently to be allowed to leave. But it was Mr Park who turned away. "How... how long will it last?" I called after him.

Mr Park stopped but didn't turn around. "That is up to you," he replied.

Au Clair de Lune was a really nice love hotel. It had a proper reception desk and a lift. Like in a regular hotel, it had an ikebana arrangement in the lobby and a small restaurant. It was not cheap—10,000 yen for five hours was the lowest figure on the tariff list. I walked up to the woman at the reception and asked for the key. She was a foreigner and handed me the keys without a word. I took the lift to the fifth floor. You may be wondering how there could have been a fifth floor when I have already told you that there were only four floors. Well, the reason is that one floor was underground. Most love hotels today make two floors underground but Au Clair de Lune was a classy place and it had only one underground floor. I hate the underground rooms. It is always the worst men who take those rooms.

"You're a classy lady," the man remarked when I entered. I was wearing my Dolce & Gabbana black dress. You can always rely on Dolce & Gabbana for the sexy smart look. He was standing by the television, smoking. He had a thick Kyushu accent.

I was too scared to look at him, so I looked at his shoes instead. To my surprise they weren't Italian, or even French but cheap Japanese imitations. I felt better immediately. He might have been a *shyacho*, bossing people around, but I was the one wearing the Louis Vuitton shoes.

"Take off your clothes and go brush your teeth," he ordered. I quickly did as he asked, remembering Mr Park's words. "And leave the bathroom door open," he ordered. As I brushed my teeth I tried to look at him in the mirror. But the room was so dark that I could not make out the expression on his face. That made me even more nervous.

Somehow I finished taking off my clothes and lay down on the bed, praying for it to end quickly. I was so tight that the man could not enter so he grew angry. "I asked for a mature woman, you are as tight as a virgin," he said.

I felt shocked at his words. No man had ever talked to me like that. I think I must have become even stiffer, for after a few tries he pushed me away in disgust and got up to go.

"No, please don't go," I cried. He ignored me and began to put on his pants. I leapt out of bed and grabbed his legs, stammering something like "no, no, please please" over and over. At last he dropped his pants and grabbed my head, pulling it up to his slowly softening erection. He made me put my lips around it and suck him until it hardened again and then just as I was about to pull away he grabbed my head and held it in position and began to move, jamming himself into my mouth again and again. My head felt swollen like the inside of a drum. I was absolutely breathless. Then suddenly he let go and I, desperate for air, pulled my head away so he ended up coming all over my hair and ears.

"I'm so sorry, I'm so sorry," I gasped, scrambling on all fours towards the Kleenex box beside the bed.

He laughed and patting my head as if I was a favourite pet, he said, "That was a first."

I made 50,000 yen that first time. And he gave me 10,000 more as a tip and made me promise to keep myself free for him whenever he came to town. I agreed wholeheartedly. I was so relieved I hadn't failed.

What did he look like, you ask me? He was good-looking, young. Maybe not. The truth is I don't remember. Even though I did see him again a few times, I don't remember his face. Or the faces of any of the men I have slept with. I remember the things some of them made me do. Yes, I remember those things. But what matters is that I was able to do those things and get paid. I gave satisfaction. I was successful. I was useful.

I don't care about the faces of the men I sleep with, or the hands that touch me. Neither face nor hands can leave a mark, for my mind is powerful enough to erase it all. Do you know why? Because when I am with them, I think of the money I will make and immediately a picture comes to life in my mind: I see a pond in the middle of rice fields. The pond is covered with lotuses and I am one of them. I feel the wind caressing me with rough hands and the coldness of the mud in which my roots have found their anchor. And I feel my body taking the shape of a beautiful delicate flower, open to the wind and the rain. My arms curl around their backs and my legs around their thighs like roots reaching into slippery soil. I become the lotus, pure and indestructible. And then I cry out and hold them even tighter.

The Wisdom of the Oyster

Now that you know how I came to be who I am, are you happy? Does my story give you an erection?

What! You ask if I have told you everything? Now I am going to get angry. I am going to leave. I don't like being insulted.

But you are right. I have left out an important chunk of my story, for it does not concern you, it concerns someone else. My heart hurts whenever I think of it. But maybe it is time to tell that part too. Maybe, telling it will make my heart lighter. I will try.

I had been working for four years and I enjoyed every minute of my life. On the outside, I was the best-dressed woman in Tokyo. Whenever I went shopping, women stared at me enviously. Everyone from the hairdresser to my husband's boss remarked on how good I looked. And on the inside I felt so strong. For in those encounters with strange men I had found an important thing about myself. I knew how to please men. I could do anything with them and they enjoyed it. Through them I discovered my power and it drew them to me like flies to syrup. So when I walked down the street in Ginza or Omotesando, they looked at me and wanted me, and I got more looks than Tomoko ever did. Even my husband noticed it and once again I found him looking at me hungrily with his head cocked a little to one side, the way he had when we first met.

And so I was happy all the time. I measured the days and weeks only by the clothes I bought and the men I had made happy.

Sometimes I went straight to the shops after a meeting with a client, the money warm in my purse and my body still tired. In the changing room I would take off my clothes, stare hard at my body to see if it had changed and then put on my gorgeous new clothes. When I came out I felt pure and new again. On days when I didn't work I used my credit card if I saw something I liked. The only dark spot on my otherwise perfect life was that Mr Park was no longer my contact. Another younger man was. His name was Crocodile.

Crocodile was the opposite of Mr Park.

Mr Park was kind, and he was intelligent. I never understood how a man so gentle ended up working with criminals. Once a month we would meet at a coffee shop in Tokyo and after he collected his share of the money we would talk. He told me funny stories about the other women he worked with and made me laugh. I felt as if we were colleagues and friends but all the time he was teaching me, training me to be careful, to think like a criminal.

"Women in your profession are rarely killed by their clients," he would always end one of his stories by saying, "they are killed by their husbands." He made me promise to tell my husband nothing and to work only three at most four times a week. That kept my price high and it prevented any of my neighbours from getting suspicious. Mr Park also made me promise not to change clothes in the house but to always change in the toilet at the station. Other women had made the mistake of telling their husbands they were doing a part-time job at a bar or restaurant. "It never works, eventually the husbands want details, a telephone number, an address, sooner or later they come to check on their wives," he would say.

Crocodile never told me what his real name was, and I never asked. All I knew was that he was Japanese, much younger than me (only a little older than my son probably), and dressed like a dandy in grey pinstriped suits and top hats. His long hair he dyed silver-grey to match his silver-grey camping caravan, the love of his life. When he called me that first time I knew that Mr Park was dead but I was too scared to ask. At home I was careful to keep to my routines and let nothing change. On my own I would probably have served my children beef every day but Mr Park's story about a woman whose husband became suspicious of her because she suddenly started serving him his favourite foods every day stopped me from making the same mistake.

I am telling you this because if Mr Park was alive today I would not have to tell you what I am going to tell you. Crocodile was the one who ruined everything. A year after Crocodile took over, he began to pressure me to do more jobs, morning and afternoon, sometimes evenings too. At first he accepted my refusals, then he began to threaten me. "If you don't do this one, I will call you at night. Maybe your husband will pick up the phone. Maybe I will come and visit your daughter when you are out." So to keep him happy, every month I agreed to one of his requests.

One warm autumn afternoon as I was hanging the laundry out to dry I heard the phone ring. It was Crocodile. He sounded irritated, and drunk. "Why don't you pick up the phone?" he demanded. "Do you want all the neighbours to know what you do as well?"

"I just came in. I was shopping," I lied.

"You're lying," he said. "It doesn't take so long to open a

161

door." I was not good at lying.

"What do you want?" I said.

"A client wants to see you tomorrow, 4 p.m." Tomorrow was Friday. I never worked on Fridays because sometimes the children came home early.

"You know why I can't do it."

"Come on, just this once. He's a really big guy, real important. Normally he won't touch anyone over seventeen, but he's heard of you."

"I'll do it next week."

"He won't wait. He's so mad about you he wants you now. I had a hard enough time persuading him to agree to wait till tomorrow. I'm with him now."

The stupid fool. Mr Park would never have promised me to someone without asking me first. I cursed him under my breath.

"All right, but this is the last time," I told him.

"You should never say last," Mr Park always said. "There is only one last, and that is death. Last is an unlucky word." I returned late the next day. It was past 7 p.m. and the house was a single spot of darkness in a street full of lighted windows. I saw it from the top of the street and felt relieved. Though I was laden with shopping bags, I ran the last part of the way. Because I was in a hurry, I didn't check the mailbox.

When I entered the hallway, Ryu was sitting on the bench in the darkness. Though he hadn't taken off his shoes, I knew he'd been there a long time. The mail was lying beside him in a neat pile.

"What... what are you doing here?" I stammered.

"Thinking," he replied. It was too dark to see his face, and his voice sounded almost normal. My first thought was that he had lost his job. People lost their jobs every day at the bank.

"Where have you been?" he asked gravely.

"Shopping," I replied, grateful for the grocery bags in my hands. "How long have you been sitting like this?"

"Two hours. Maybe more," he replied.

"I'm sorry," I said sincerely, sitting down beside him. It was nice sitting there in the dark with our backs against the cold stone wall. I felt closer to him then than I had felt in a long time. In the darkness I reached for his hand but he immediately pulled away from me.

"Is everything all right at the bank?" I asked gently, still thinking he'd been fired.

"I suppose so. I was just feeling tired so I took the afternoon off and came home," he replied. "I didn't realise there would be no-one home."

I said nothing, but inside my head I was cursing Crocodile.

Ryu and I sat like that in the darkness for a few more minutes. Then I said, "I better start the dinner. The children should be here any time. Why don't you come inside and I'll fix you a drink?"

His head jerked up in surprise and he looked at me sharply. For Ryu never drank at home. Then, reluctantly, he nodded. Then it was my turn to be surprised at myself. I should have remembered he never drank at home. What made me treat him the way I treated my other clients?

We were saved from further awkwardness by the arrival of the children. But then the evening became surreal. I felt as if I was looking at my life from the outside—the way I watched television sometimes while doing the ironing. Everything went the way it was meant to. Ryu, who was always silent anyway, buried himself behind his newspaper, while I prepared the dinner and listened to Haruka's endless chatter about school and friends. My Aki-chan, quiet like Ryu, switched on the television and watched it through his curtain of messy long

163

hair. I cut the onions and ginger and fried them, adding the sake, shoyu and meat when they were brown. Only I could not smell or taste anything; for I was outside it all, watching and waiting for something to break.

It happened after dinner. Ryu suddenly put down his newspaper. "I am going up," he announced, then, holding out a white envelope, he added, "This was in the mailbox. Your bank wants to offer you a gold credit card. Congratulations. They think you are a valuable customer."

The plate slipped out of my hand and landed on the floor but strangely it didn't break. Ryu went calmly up the stairs to our bedroom. The children looked surprised but said nothing. They quickly finished up and excused themselves from the table.

I waited a long time downstairs. I cleaned the dirty dishes twice, wiped the table three times and then mopped the floor of the kitchen. All the while the white envelope stared at me accusingly from its position on the corner of the table. I longed for a smoke but didn't have the energy to go out and buy one. At last I pulled out the letter the bank had sent me. It wasn't much of a letter, just one of those mass mail things inviting their customers to get a credit card. But at the bottom the bank manager, Maruyama-san, had written me a note. It was a nice note, very kind, but it killed the last bit of hope left inside me: "Congratulations, your account is in very good health. So happy that my friends were able to help you with your financial difficulties." Ryu was a banker, he would know what those words meant. Maybe he had already called Sumitomo bank and asked Maruyama-san about me.

I thought of a thousand lies and rejected them all. Then, like the top of a volcano emerging in the late evening sunlight from its cover of summer clouds, the truth became apparent to me. I could not lie to Ryu. Though, in our marriage, the words themselves had grown fewer and fewer, no untrue words had passed between us. I could not change that. I would not change it. For, peace and happiness, I realised, were two different things. Happiness was like the bubbles on the surface of dirty dishwater. Peace was the water itself. Water washed away all dirt, it made things pure and whole again. If I let the water run out of my life, there would be no bubbles. And then what would be left?

So I decided to say nothing.

The days passed with deadly slowness. I called Crocodile and told him my husband suspected me and so he shouldn't call me till I called him. "All right," he growled, "but don't wait too long or you will have no clients left."

Every day Ryu waited patiently for me to explain myself. He made a point of coming home before eight in the evening and eating dinner with the family. After his bath he would sit in the living room and his eyes would follow me like hungry dogs. It was horrible. I longed to confess, to tell Ryu everything, to explain, to be forgiven. And yet, whenever I imagined myself doing so, I saw in my mind his eyes turning away from me in disgust. So my words stayed in my stomach, growing heavier each day. I imagined I was an oyster and my silence was a pearl. If I waited long enough, maybe my pearl would be so big and so valuable that Ryu could sell it and we would be rich. Then I would not have to worry about wanting to buy new clothes. The big thing that was destroying my life would become a small thing of little consequence and we would laugh about it together, Ryu and I.

Days became weeks and more than a month passed. Still I waited for the moment when he would understand my silence and his eyes would turn away from me. In my mind I had imagined it so many times that I felt utterly numb. Still I clung to the image of the oyster silently preparing his surprise, turning the dirt that had invaded its home into a thing of incredible value.

Then one day Ryu surprised me. He came home from the office at six in the evening, waving two tickets in my face. For the first time in weeks, he smiled. "Pack your bags," he said, "Friday we go on holiday, you and I."

He could not have surprised me more. "But... but what about your job?"

"I have taken three months' leave," he replied.

"Three months?" I was stunned.

"I can, of course go back earlier," he said.

I didn't believe him. No-one gave anyone three months' leave in Japan. "Are you sure you haven't lost your job?" I asked suspiciously.

Ryu laughed. "Of course not. I told them my wife is sick and that I need to nurse her back to health again."

I frowned. I was not sick at all. I would have told him everything right then, I was so angry, but he didn't give me the chance. "This is all my fault," he said, hugging me to his chest, "I left you alone too much. You were so young when we married, naturally you got into trouble. Just tell me what your problem is and I will find you a doctor who can fix it. If you have debts, just tell me how much and I will pay it. I promise I won't be angry. If we have to we can sell the house. We don't really need so much space."

And when I still wouldn't speak, he continued, "It's okay. Don't say anything now. When we are alone, you and I will have the time to talk."

"But... but what about the children?" I stammered when at last I found my tongue.

"My mother is coming to look after them."

My face must have stiffened because Ryu hastened to add, "Don't worry. We will be gone by the time she gets here."

*

The problem with Ryu was that he was no romantic. Gentle he was, and clever. But he had no imagination and so he could not be romantic. I think people with no imagination are automatically good. They cannot be anything else. And they cannot imagine another's problems or their badness. I don't know what Ryu told himself about my secret bank account. Maybe he had decided that the money came from him, from his salary which I had saved and diverted into my personal account. Maybe he decided that I was sick or depressed and that is why I had stolen the money. Maybe he felt that all I needed was a little cheering up and then the trouble would pass and everything would become normal again.

If Ryu had had even a little imagination, he would have taken me to Europe, to Paris or Rome, Milan or London. He would have made me drink lots of wine and told me he loved me and then things would have been different. Instead, he took me to the spa town of Yufuin, in the mountains not far from Beppu where his mother lived.

If you have never been to Kyushu you'd better not waste your money. It is a hot, green hell. All you have there are volcanoes and boiling hot water full of sulphur that seeps out of cracks in the earth's crust. On top of these hot springs, multi-million yen hotels and ryokans have been built—that offer you red, green, yellow, or turquoise-coloured water; you can take your pick. Some of the onsens are so hot you cannot get inside and these are called "hells". People cook food in them. One time, on our honeymoon at his mother's home, Ryu took me to eat in a "hell" spa in Beppu. After we had bathed, we wore our kimonos and went into an elegant Japanese-style dining room where the food was already on the table. It looked delicious, as good as anything you would find in a Tokyo restaurant. But it tasted awful—watery, and with a strong smell of rotten eggs. I could not eat it. Yet all around me were entire families eating the elegantly presented food with their chopsticks and seeming to enjoy it! It was the first time I looked at the world and wondered whether it was mad or if it was me.

But natives of Kyushu have an almost mystical faith in their Kyushu "hells" and their onsens. They believe the waters can cure all sorts of ailments from eczema to nervous disorders—especially women's nervous problems like hysteria or depression. That is why Ryu took me to Kyushu. Perhaps he thought the magic waters of his native land would take care of my illness.

From the moment we got into the plane I grew increasingly nervous. I had a premonition that I would not be returning to Tokyo in the near future. And though I knew such a thing was impossible, I couldn't shake off the feeling and that made me very fidgety. Out of the corner of my eye I looked at my husband. He looked relaxed and happy, just the way a man going on holiday was supposed to look. "How long are we going for?" I asked sharply. I had already asked the question several times but each time Ryu had answered vaguely.

"I told you—as long as we want," Ryu replied, again avoiding my question.

"What does that mean," I grumbled, "how can I plan what clothes to bring for 'as long as you want'?"

"Then don't plan. If you run out of clothes I will buy you some more," he said.

Silenced, I retreated into my thoughts. But the more I

thought about it, the more my nervousness grew.

At Beppu airport, Ryu went straight to the Yamada rent-a-car agency counter. By the time we finished the formalities and got into the car it was almost one in the afternoon. Again I asked, "Where are we going? Are we going to stay in your mother's house?"

Ryu's mother's house was in a village not far from Beppu. It was a horrible place, without even a single shop to buy coffee.

"Of course not. That would not be a holiday," he replied. Still he wouldn't tell me where we were going. As we drove out of the city towards the highway I looked longingly at the shops. The urge to buy was almost overwhelming. Even on the highway, Ryu drove slowly, cautiously. As a result we arrived at Yufuin as the sun was setting.

The ryokan Ryu took me to was one of the oldest ones in Yufuin. As soon as we entered the charming wooden entrance we were swallowed by another Japan, the Japan of foreign tourists and the rich. It cost 31,000 yen per person for a one-night stay. For the two of us it would come to 62,000 yen! What was my husband thinking? I was shocked but Ryu just smiled calmly as if it were nothing. I thought of all the beautiful clothes I could have bought for that price even in a small city like Kumamoto and felt angry at him for wasting money.

But when I saw the Japanese-style room, the brand-new tatami still smelling of late autumn sunshine and the tokonoma with the simple blue vase carrying a single flame-coloured Momiji (maple) branch, my anger vanished. Ryu immediately took possession of the engawa, disappearing behind his newspaper. Meanwhile, I unpacked and looked around the room, admiring the details—the texture of the walls, the woodwork of cranes flying over a field of autumn grass, the washi lamp. Suddenly, Ryu emerged from behind his newspaper and asked me to prepare some tea. I arranged our things in the cupboard not wanting to destroy the simple beauty of the room and then took out the tea set, admiring the celadon cups and the iron tea pot.

I tell you this because I want you to understand what happened next. As I waited for the water to come to a boil, I suddenly began to feel lighter, as if summer had returned and I had just thrown off my heavy woolen clothes. And then, just as suddenly, I felt something inside me change, like furniture rearranging itself, not just my mind but my entire body became different. I was no longer me. I became someone else, someone that matched the seamless beauty of the room. One more thing became clear to me, this person who was sitting in the beautiful room, making tea for her husband, really and truly loved the man she was making tea for. The phrase "revealing one's heart in the preparation of tea" suddenly leapt into my mind. I had first encountered it in a documentary on tea ceremony on television. At the time it had made little sense to me but now the full power and beauty of the words hit me. As I poured the boiling water over the fresh green leaves, I tried to put my feelings into the tea. It struck me then that the only man I had ever made tea for was Ryu. And as I poured the fragrant green liquid into the cup, I swore to myself that no matter what I did or who touched my breasts, I would only ever make tea for the man sitting in the covered verandah reading his newspaper.

The peace lasted till dinner. Dressed in the hotel's yukatas we joined a group of similarly dressed holidaymakers going to dinner. We greeted the others politely and as a group went laughingly in search of the dining room. One man in the group kept looking back at me. He looked strangely familiar and seemed to feel the same way, for at the bottom of the stairs he turned and asked Ryu and me politely, "Forgive me for my memory is not so good any more, have we met somewhere before?" He had a strong Kyushu accent.

"I don't think so. I am from Beppu originally but we have been living in Tokyo for the last twenty years," my husband replied. The man nodded and said no more but his eyes went to my breasts and remained there. I had to clench my hands at my sides to stop them from trying to cover my breasts. How I hated them, those two big pumpkins dangling on my chest. I wished I could tear them off and make them disappear.

We entered the restaurant and were immediately led to separate alcoves by the kimono-clad staff. The dining room was really beautiful—large and airy with glass everywhere. Outside, the forest was cleverly lit up so that one felt as if one was picnicking among the trees. It was the last I saw of the man and his group but for me the magic was broken. I was no longer a part of the world of the ryokan. I was the leaf that had fallen from the tree, the broken chair, the soiled yukata, the outsider. I ate the delicious dinner without tasting anything. That night when my husband reached for me, I felt like a prostitute, not a wife. I could not sleep. I kept thinking of the middle-aged man on the stairs. Had he really been one of my clients? And what about the others—what if one them had been a colleague of my husband? I looked at my husband's salt and pepper head lying peacefully between my breasts and burned with shame.

Luckily we didn't see the man at breakfast but I was so nervous I was sweating uncontrollably all through the meal. What if he came up to us and denounced me in front of my husband? What would I do? Even though I knew such a thing could not happen, for the man had probably been with his wife, I could not help imagining it again and again. Perhaps somewhere inside my heart I wanted it to happen. Then the words that were turning to stones in my stomach would leave me and I could enjoy life again.

In the daylight the dining room looked even more beautiful than it had the previous night. A filtered green sunlight bathed the room in tranquility. Suddenly I couldn't wait to get away. I felt like I was in a hospital waiting room and all the kimono-clad guests were patients waiting to meet the doctor. I am not sick, I wanted to shout, I just want to be happy. But the words that were turning to stones in my stomach made me feel full and I could not eat any of the delicious breakfast the hotel had prepared for us. Ryu sensed my nervousness. "What is the matter?" he asked. "Aren't you happy with this?"

"Of course I am," I replied, bending my head and forcing some food into my mouth.

Only when we were in the car again did I relax. But thanks to that stupid man I have no memory of the ryokan, the only expensive place Ryu ever took me to. And I forgot to ask Ryu how he had known about the place, and why he had taken me there. Perhaps if I had, this story's end would have been different. I would not have been here, telling this to you, and you would not have been dying.

Yes, you heard correctly. I do not want to kill you, for you are kind and generous. But I am compelled to do so. I have no other choice. That numbness in your legs, the pins and needles beginning in your hands have nothing to do with the after-effects of sex. If you try to move them now, you will see that it is impossible.

You look towards the door nervously even as you laugh with your mouth. Do you think I am joking? Here, smell your glass. Now do you believe me? I have never lied to you. I have always told you the truth. You should not have asked me to tell you about myself. But you insisted.

I would really like to be in your place, to feel the life leave me slowly and know that tomorrow I will not have to plan or organize any more. Then I would really know the difference between being dead and alive. I sometimes get confused, you know. For isn't one most alive when everyone thinks one is dead? And can one not be dead when everyone thinks you are alive? For that is exactly my experience. Wait till you hear the rest of my story and you will understand. There is not much left.

To Aso-san

For five days Ryu drove us through the desolate countryside of Aso-Kuju national park. It was the middle of November and nature was preparing for winter. Every night the frost would turn the fallen leaves to silver and in the morning, when we got into the car, fog covered the ground, so thick and white that it felt as if we were driving through cotton wool. The fog was like a wall, so real that I would roll down my window and try to touch it. But my hand simply disappeared. I could still feel it at the end of my arm, but I couldn't see it any more.

But by around nine thirty or ten, a wind came along, a wind so strong that it rattled the branches of the trees. The fog disappeared and autumn colours, brown and gold and silver, appeared. The ground was bare and dark as the rice had all been cut. Hoarfrost had turned the cut rice stalks into silver needles that clinked under the feet like broken glass when one walked on it. But by noon the sun appeared and the sky would be a fierce and brilliant blue, and miraculously, the meadows were still green. It was peaceful to drive through the endless rolling hills. The sudden disappearance of the fog was always a shock, and each day I waited for it, to discover the world anew.

Every night we stopped at a different ryokan and bathed in onsens, hidden in nature, sometimes twice or three times a day. The onsen towns we stayed in were one more beautiful than the next, but we never passed a single clothing store. That is how poor Kyushu is. But by the third day something strange happened to me, I no longer searched each village we came to for a shop. I can't say I stopped thinking of clothes, but the fire that was inside me every time I thought of a shop had died down. Whether this was the effect of the onsens or whether it was the beauty of the environment I cannot say. But I certainly felt different. Ryu was also nicer. Though he still didn't talk very much, I was impressed with how well he had planned the trip and how he took care of me. For example, he had even thought of bringing a small blanket to cover my legs in the car, for in the mornings, when we got in, it was really chilly. And each night, though tired from all the driving, he would reach for me and hold me tight, and then he would kiss me with his tongue and reach into me with all his might as if he were searching for something. Or maybe he was just playing fireman, trying to put out the evil burning inside me.

Talking of firemen, I will share something with you which you will like. Remember, you asked me if I had any clients who were special? Well there was this one man, let us call him X, who I cannot forget. He was old, seventy-eight, one of my oldest clients. But he was very fit and climbed mountains once a week. After we'd been together a few times he invited me to come to his apartment. The building he lived in, a public housing building right in the heart of Tokyo, in the Bancho area, was very modern and fairly new as well—dark grey concrete with silver pipes piercing the walls. I began to go to him regularly twice a month on Tuesday mornings, to his small one-room apartment in the public housing complex in Yonbancho.

But why I tell you this is because my client was a fireman and he liked to play games, especially fire-related games. He told me that all firemen ever read, as they waited for fires to break out, was manga-porn. They exchanged their manga magazines and discussed the stories. And they told their own versions of what was published. It was the stories he missed most, he told me, proceeding to tie me up with a fire hose, my legs spread wide before me. Then he would read me his favourite manga and make me take the position of his favourite pictures. But he was always so gentle and funny and made me feel like I was a great actress. The single room with a bed and a small dining table became all sorts of things—a ship, a burning high-rise, and by the time I left, the room was awash in fire and water. I went to him on Tuesday mornings twice a month for a year, and to be frank, I looked forward to our meetings. Till one day, a hot, hot day in August, there was an ambulance outside the building and four fire engines. I looked up to where his apartment was. The window was open and a few stray wisps of smoke could still be seen. I would have liked to go to his funeral, to see all the other firemen gathered around in their uniforms.

On the fourth day, Ryu brought me to Aso-san, Kyushu's one live volcano. First, he showed me the caldera—its sharp sides dropping with knife-like precision into the valley below. I looked up, steam rose from the mouth of the volcano to the left. A chill ran down my spine. One day it would erupt and all the homes, all the fields would be gone, covered in ash.

"How can they live there," I burst out, "not knowing when they will lose everything?"

"You talk like a foreigner," Ryu said, looking at me coldly. "Life is not about what you can buy, it is about doing. The two are very different things."

So he knew, I thought, and something exploded inside me. "I never said anything about buying, but it is plain madness to make a rice field under a live volcano," I said sharply.

"The volcano is part of the natural cycle of the field. Only when the field is destroyed can it be rebuilt," Ryu said calmly. "As a Japanese you should understand that."

"And what about you? Working for an American company, making me learn English and bake brownies for your American colleagues. Is that Japanese?" I asked.

Suddenly I could no longer stop myself. I said horrible things. I made my words into stones and aimed carefully at all the sensitive places on my husband's body and heart. I told him about the kimono. But I blamed it on his mother's meanness, giving me a stained kimono all nicely folded to look new. I told him about my mother's present and how I hid it from him. I told him about the sales and the credit card. I blamed him, for never being there, for never talking to me. For leaving me alone in a cheap little street full of eyes and ears and not a single friendly heart. I didn't tell him about pachinko or the men. That I knew I could not ever speak of.

All the time I spoke, Ryu stared impassively at the rice fields, refusing to meet my eyes, and when I finally stopped, he said calmly, "Shall we go?"

"Where to?" I was stunned, exhausted. I wanted to crawl into a bed and sleep for a week. But I also wanted to hear Ryu, to know what he thought. But Ryu was good at making people wait. He knew how to wear them down with waiting, just like his mother.

"To Aso-san," he replied, jerking his chin towards the volcano.

We drove down the twisting road into the rice fields and then up again, through pastures now turning yellow and brown, to the top of the volcano. Around the volcano the earth was the colour of dried blood and the air smelled bad. Nothing grew there. Every day poisonous gases escaped from the volcano. I took deep breaths, sucking those fumes into my lungs. Looking over the crater's edge at the emerald green lake at the centre, I thought how nice it would be to fall inside. The water was such a beautiful colour. Two columns of steam rose like tornadoes from the centre of the lake, getting bigger and bigger as they reached the sky. If I let myself fall, the lake would swallow my miserable life, I thought, and turn the unsaid words that were like rocks inside me into precious diamonds. My soul would rise to heaven on a cloud of poisonous gas to be judged and sent to hell forever. But some day someone would find the diamonds and be made rich.

Without being aware of it, my eyes fell on my husband. He was the only one who would really miss me, I realised suddenly. The children wouldn't, they had their own lives now. But Ryu's life was me and our home. I turned to Ryu, my mouth opening to tell him what I had just realised, but to my surprise I saw that he was speaking.

"When I was eight," I heard him say, "my father brought me here. He was dying then. The cancer that had begun in his prostate had spread all over. I do not know if he knew that he was dying or whether he only suspected. But he told me that we humans were like volcanoes. Every once in a while we would erupt and all sorts of evil things would pour out of us and try to destroy all life around us. But love was stronger than the volcano. Love was like the rain that washed away the ash and turned it into something life-giving and life-sustaining. Love was stronger than death, he told me, never ever forget that."

"And what has that got to do with us?" I asked rudely. I was determined not to understand.

"It means that I will never leave you," he said simply. "No matter what."

We got into the car and began our return. That night we

stayed at Kurokawa onsen, on the edge of Aso national park. It was a beautiful old onsen town with many great onsens and ryokan. Ours was named Ikoi, like the fish. For the first time in a month, I was able to eat. Ryu watched me clean my plate of food and smiled. That night we made love as if it were the first and last time—like two people without a past and without a future—madly, wildly, with no reserve. Afterwards, sleep, which had been a fugitive for the last few weeks, took possession of my mind and body and so I slept deeply and dreamlessly till nine the next morning. When my eyes opened, Ryu was looking down at me fully dressed.

"There is someone I want you to meet today," he said, "someone who was like a father to me after my own died. He has a special character but don't be afraid, I will be with you."

I sat up quickly, clutching the sheet to my naked body. "Is he here? I am not dressed."

Ryu laughed. "No, he isn't here. He doesn't travel much any more. So today, we go to him."

We drove and we drove, going ever deeper into the Kyushu countryside, to a land where there were no shops, no family marts, no apartments in high-rises, just rice fields with dry, broken stalks and tumbledown old houses heaped one on top of the other. The trees were the biggest things there. I must have fallen asleep because when my eyes opened again the car had stopped and Ryu was nowhere to be seen. The thought came to me that he had abandoned me. I pushed open the door in a panic and shouted Ryu's name.

The car was in the driveway of an old temple. To my right was a zen garden in sand and stone, and to the left a giant matsu tree guarded the entrance to the old wooden temple.

"Ryu-chan!" I shouted again. "Where are you?"

No-one answered. The house looked as if it were sleeping

and the zen garden was as still as a painting.

Do you know Japanese Zen gardens? I think they are horrible things, especially when one is alone. For there is nothing alive inside them. As I looked at the three black and white stones, the leafless cherry tree and the straight lines carefully carved into the sand I felt I had been transported to the place in purgatory where souls awaited judgement. At that moment, I couldn't help but feel that the unknown man inside the house, who Ryu had brought me to meet, was already judging me and finding me worthless.

Perhaps I should have run away then. I must admit I considered it, but where could I have run to in that empty land?

Invisible

At last my husband came out of the temple entrance, followed by a bent old woman. "There you are!" I exclaimed, relieved. "I was looking for you."

"You were deep asleep," Ryu answered, looking a little puzzled by the warmth of my welcome. "I didn't want to disturb you. Let me introduce you, this is Okaa-san."

The old woman who came forward seemed old enough to be Ryu's grandmother rather than his mother. She was thin and bent like a bow and her hair covered by a peasant scarf was as white as snow. Like all country people she was wearing an apron over her clothes but I could see that the clothes were old and patched. Then I looked into her face and was surprised. For her skin, though lined and wrinkled, was pure and unmarked, incredibly youthful in fact.

"You looked so tired. Are you feeling better now?" she asked. She smiled at me kindly and I liked her immediately.

"My husband had to go to the head temple in Shikoku today," she said. "But he will be back the day after tomorrow. You both will stay with us till he returns?"

We both turned to Ryu. He was looking at his watch and in that instant I knew what he was going to do. I then looked at the old woman to see if she had noticed too. She had, and the smile she gave me was full of sympathy.

"Okaa-san, I am sorry, I have to catch the evening plane,

next time," Ryu said, looking at her and not at me.

"What a pity. It's so beautiful here," I said impulsively. The next minute I regretted the words that had slipped out of my mouth for Ryu, looking at me distantly as if he were already on the plane, smiled. I realised I had been manipulated all along.

"Of course you should stay. You could keep mother company till her husband comes back," he said as he went to the back of the car and took out my suitcase.

"Ryu-chan, when will you come and get me?" I whispered anxiously, following him. He didn't answer.

I asked the question again, a little louder this time.

"Soon, as soon as... I finish my work." He would not look at me.

"But you will come back?" I insisted.

"Of course," he said strongly, pulling me into a short hard embrace.

Then he quickly said goodbye to Okaa-san and drove away.

I don't blame Ryu for leaving me like that. Not then and not now. He had a family and a job to consider. In his place I would have done the same thing. But after he left I felt terrified, convinced that I would never see him again. Everything around me felt strange and unfamiliar, as if I had indeed been transported to another planet.

I don't know how it is in your country but in Japan, the city and the countryside are two very different worlds. In the past they may have been part of the same world, but now they are more like two separate worlds joined only by the finest of threads. Anything can make those threads break and then the two worlds will drift apart.

Take, for example, space. On the surface it seems that space is the same everywhere you go. It is the sky, the air you breathe,

the place you live, the clouds, everything that is empty and yet surrounds your body. Maybe you think that sky is sky, space is space, you either have more of it or less but basically it doesn't change much—whether you are in Tokyo or in Kyushu. But I tell you, you are wrong. The sky is not the same in Tokyo and in Kyushu. The clouds, the air, the colour, the smell, the way the scenery marries the sky—everything is different. And one more thing, space or the lack of it can change your heart. That is why the country and the city have become two completely different worlds.

Space in the countryside has little or no value. It is about loneliness, poverty and cold. In the city it is the opposite. People live one on top of the other and so a person's worth is measured by the amount of space he has at his disposal. The head of a company or a bank for example has a large office while those under him have little cubicles and those even further down have only desks. The shyacho knows he is important because everywhere he goes the space around him remains constant as those with him keep a respectful distance. But for the others there is never enough space, not in a city like Tokyo. But we humans can grow used to living with very little space quite quickly and a time comes when too much space makes us scared.

That is exactly what happened to me that first night in the temple.

Okaa-san had given me their best guest room, a twenty-four tatami room with beautifully painted fusuma situated to the right of the main temple hall. It was a huge space made even larger by the fact that the ceiling was the giant vaulting ceiling of the temple main hall itself. As I lay down on the futon I could not help wondering how one single human could possibly fill up all that empty space. I closed my eyes but sleep would not come to me. All around the house, the night was an unforgiving uniform black, dense and solid as a mountain or a cement wall. I stared up at the old wooden beams black with age and felt myself reduced to the size and significance of a worm. The space pressed down upon me, heavy and oppressive. I felt like I had been put into a box and that even if I screamed and screamed no-one would hear me. I grew angry. How could anyone bear that much empty space? Why couldn't they fill it with noise and light as we did in the city? Why couldn't they at least put some more warm live bodies into that darkness. I wished Ryu had been there beside me, as he had always been, and ended up cursing him and all his ancestors in despair. I opened and shut my eyes and felt no difference to the quality of darkness. And then I began to get really scared. The night was utterly silent, no sound anywhere, nothing moved—not a leaf fell or a wild animal prowled. I felt like I was the only person alive in the world.

As the hours slowly trickled by and I still could not sleep, the feeling that I was in reality all alone grew into certainty. The old lady was so old and frail she could die any time in her sleep, I reasoned. Maybe she had died already and that's why everything felt so still. Would I starve to death before they came and found me? Was that the punishment Ryu had had in mind for me? As the night progressed, the room developed icy teeth. In spite of the futon I became so cold that I could not move. I thought longingly of my cosy eight-tatami bedroom in Chofu. Shutting my eyes tight, I prayed that when I reopened them I would be back in my own bed, Ryu's feet sticking into my ribs, the walls within touching distance. But in the morning when my eyes opened I realised that it was the hard floor that was poking into my ribs, not Ryu's feet.

I sat up, determined to call Ryu and insist he take me back

to Tokyo. But the room looked quite different in the daylight. Sunlight filtering through the shoji spilled onto the tatami, highlighting the many different colours hidden in the straw. The painted fusuma, a mountainous landscape with a tranquil lake beside which a woman sat with pen and ink in her hand while nearby two children played with a kite, also looked different, somehow more alive. On the adjacent wall two peasants engaged in a conversation beside a spray of autumn grass. Beyond them an eagle perched on a cliff overlooking a plum tree. After I had looked at them all for some time I realised that the room no longer felt empty. In fact it felt quite the opposite—full of the feelings of the people in those paintings and maybe even of the hands that painted them.

Quickly I dressed and made the bed. My tiny bag looked like an alien creature in the centre of that big old room. I pushed it into a corner behind the table. Then, unable to bear the emptiness of my surroundings, I pushed open the fusuma leading onto the wooden corridor.

And then I got my second surprise.

It wasn't a very large garden but it was long, extending the entire length of the building. It had all the usual things a garden has, a collection of unusual black and white rocks, a waterfall, a lake with moss-covered islands in it, a big stone lantern. The waterfall broke into tiny silver droplets on the backs of three smooth, dark brown stones and then flowed calmly onwards around clumps of autumn grasses or moss-covered islands. Behind the water and stones, the forest rose in layers, one after the other, going from yellow to orange to dark evergreen.

I cannot tell you the names of all the trees and plants in that garden, except for the momiji with its flame-coloured five-pointed leaves which I recognized. And even if I had been able to tell you all their names, it would not have helped you see what I saw. For that morning I was lucky. Perhaps because the gods were smiling at me or because of my lack of sleep, I didn't look at the garden with just my eyes but with my mind and with my body. Yes, my body too, for a true garden speaks not just to the mind but to the body also. With my mind I saw the garden as a living, breathing space—a place full of stillness and movement. I saw how the movement of the water started as energy flying in all directions and then grew still, just as a thought enters the brain, agitates it, and then gets absorbed into the mind, leaving the surface calm again. A leaf stirring in the breeze took on a life and a meaning of its own. And when I looked up at the mountain, and realised that the garden was as much a part of the mountain as it was of the house, I felt new spaces open inside me too. I was a part of what I saw, I realised. The tightness in my body began to fade and a lightness replaced it. My body felt released, as if the ropes that had tied it up into a tiny package had suddenly disappeared.

I will tell you frankly, up until then I was no lover of gardens. The only beauty I had ever found had been in clothes. Unlike the other mothers in Haruka's school, I had never taken guided tours of the gardens of Tokyo or studied the tea ceremony in the tea houses inside the gardens. I hadn't taken any ikebana classes either. The only "gardens" I knew were the concrete-filled playgrounds I took my children to when they were little. But as I looked out at that garden I was struck by two things: first, that what I was looking at was not simply a garden but something more like a person, or maybe the map of a person's life, with moments of beauty and moments of ugliness, and fast moments and moments of stillness. Second, that the life the garden spoke of was a good one, for everything in it had a purpose. There was nothing extra in that garden, nothing that could have been thrown away without destroying the harmony of the rest. As a result there was no crowding, everything had a space of its own, a space to breathe and be itself.

I must have spent nearly twenty minutes standing there in a kind of trance before I became aware of sounds, dishes and things being moved around not very far away. Imagining a delicious breakfast being prepared for me, I turned away from the garden at last. There in the main hall of the temple, was the old lady, neatly dressed and freshly bathed, placing freshly cooked rice and fruits on the altar.

"*Ohaiyoogosaimasu*," she greeted me, lighting some incense in a bowl. "I was just finishing the offering. Your breakfast is waiting for you in your room, I will be with you in a little while."

"No, please take your time," I said politely. "I can wait till you are done and we can eat together."

"No, no, my child," the priest's wife told me kindly, "you must be hungry. I still have the prayer to do."

"You mean to say you are a priest too?" I asked, surprised.

"No, no. Only when my husband is away," she said, laughing. "The gods have to be fed and talked to every day. So they know they are not forgotten."

I stared at the statue surrounded by food and flowers and incense and then sat down on my knees beside Okaa-san. "*Hanya Shingyo Mita Hara...*" As Okaa-san began to chant, I folded my hands. The smell of the incense and fresh rice made me feel at once peaceful and sleepy, as if I were a child in my mother's lap. My eyes closed.

My eyes opened with the tolling of the bell. Okaa-san stood up slowly and helped me up, for my legs had gone to sleep. Then she took me back to my room where a beautifully prepared breakfast of rice, fresh tofu, steamed sesame cakes and vegetables awaited me. It was absolutely delicious and I finished it quickly. When it was over, she entered again with a tea pot and a box and made me a tea so delicious it made the ryokan staff seem like amateurs. When I complimented her, she shrugged it off saying, "The water from the sacred spring in the back is what makes the tea special."

"A sacred spring?" I questioned, intrigued.

"Yes, indeed it is older than the temple itself which is 650 years old. The spring is probably why the temple was built."

"Can I go and see it?" I asked eagerly.

"Of course, I'll show you the path later," she replied, smiling kindly.

I thanked her profusely and offered to wash up but she wouldn't hear of it.

"Today you relax. Tomorrow I will let you help me," she said, chuckling.

So I wandered back to the garden and sat on the veranda for a while, enjoying the sunshine, not thinking of anything much, conscious of the food changing inside my stomach as digestion got under way. The sunshine felt wonderful and suddenly I found myself thinking that it would not be so bad to spend a little time here doing nothing. Then, as I was getting tired of being alone, Okaa-san appeared once again and sat down next to me. She brought with her a basket of rice wafers, light and still warm from the wok in which they had been fried, and some dried kaki, persimmon. We ate the fresh rice wafers in silence, staring out at the garden.

"It is good to sit down, isn't it, before a sight like this?"

"So it is," I agreed.

"With each passing day, my love for this garden only grows."

I was silent. I knew just how she felt but it scared me. This was not my home. I didn't like the idea of loving something that did not belong to me.

"I hope you will be happy with us," Okaa-san said, her voice breaking into my thoughts. "Were you ill for a long time?"

"Ill?" I looked at her in surprise. It was the first time I was hearing myself being described as ill. "I am not ill. Does it look like I am?"

"No, no. Of course not, but your illness... that's why you are here, aren't you?"

"Yes, of course. But I am totally well now," I said tightly. How dare anyone call me ill!

"Yes of course," the old lady instantly agreed, "you look very good, very rested. I think our home suits you."

I stood up abruptly. "I'm going for a walk," I said.

Okaa-san looked a little frightened but she nodded. "Go right from the gate and after you pass the field with the blue gate just turn left beside the bamboo grove. There is a lovely walking path through the fields which ends at Nakada-san's house. If you see her, please give her my best wishes. From Nakada-san's the road will bring you straight back here. If you get lost, just ask anyone for Myorinji temple, they will guide you."

"Of course, I will. Thank you," I said a little more warmly, feeling bad for my show of temper.

I met no-one on my walk and was grateful for it, for as I was walking, the word "illness" kept mocking me. What had Ryu said to the old lady? If Ryu had appeared in front of me then, I think I would have hit him. All his beautiful words, all his kindness had meant nothing then? I was so angry I think I could have shouted at anyone who came before me. But the charm of a forest is that one is almost always alone and therefore there is no-one to be angry with. So by the time I emerged onto the rice terraces, some of my anger had dissipated. A city girl, I had never seen rice terraces before and the sight of them filled me with amazement. There were hundreds of them cut neatly like steps into the hillside. Late autumn rice was still growing in some of the fields and others had fruit trees heavy with oranges. In between the fields, bamboo grew in pale green tufts and every once in a while the many shades of yellow was broken by a sprawling black-roofed farmhouse.

A small wooden bench beside a plaque on which was inscribed "Historic rice fields" caught my eye. I went over and sat down and began to read. When I had finished, I looked at the "historic rice fields" which, according to the plaque, had existed for over one thousand years, and felt incredibly small. Then I thought of my delicious breakfast and the smell of the cooked rice in the temple and a weight inside me suddenly lifted. Tokyo began to feel small and distant. The shops felt far away and the money and the clothes sitting in my secret cupboard felt far-off too. This view, these rice fields, felt real. Perhaps I had been sick, I admitted. But the thought hardly created a ripple.

When I returned, another giant meal was waiting for me. I was tired and hungry but after having eaten my fill I could not stop myself from asking the questions inside me. Who lived in the village? Where were the young people? How did the old ones survive? Okaa-san grew animated and then sad as she described how the young had all left for the city fifty or sixty years ago. "Now they only come at obon or during harvest to help their old parents," she finished.

"It must have been hard for all of you," I said, "when the children went away."

Okaa-san shrugged. "Children are like birds, they have to fly. One day they will come back. My fear is that if they don't come in time, there will be nothing to come back to."

Okaa-san's words stayed with me as I dozed on the wooden verandah in front of my room, pretending to read. It was hard to imagine the countryside disappearing but when I thought of the untilled fields I had seen and the houses with the roofs caved in I knew that Okaa-san was right. What if the old people died before the young came back? What will happen to Japan then? But my eyes soon closed and in this way, the afternoon flew by and before I knew it, the sun had set and I awoke feeling cold. Then Okaa-san arrived with a pot of hot tea and some waraabi mochi coated in brown sugar syrup. I had never been so pampered in my life. Then she bustled off to light the fire in the kitchen and cook our dinner. I retreated to my room but it was so cold that I hurriedly joined Okaa-san in the kitchen. She smiled when I entered and showed me to a little alcove protected by a curtain. There a steaming hot bath awaited me.

And so the days passed quickly.

As soon as I awoke, I would go and help Okaa-san clean the temple. Then I would have breakfast (alone, as Okaa-san had already eaten hers much earlier) and work in the garden or help with the cleaning of the temple and graveyard. A little before lunch, I went into the kitchen and helped Okaa-san prepare the lunch.

Okaa-san, of course, only cooked shojin ryori, the simple vegetarian food eaten by priests. But there was nothing simple about how she cooked it. In fact, it was the most complicated food I had ever seen. The tools she used were also rather magical and as I watched her work I felt I was watching a good fairy making magical potions to heal humans. Sometimes she cooked things I had tasted before—but she cooked them with such delicacy and love that they tasted quite different from those I had had. Other times she cooked vegetables and grains I had never ever seen. When I became familiar with the tools and how they worked, I began to help her with the things that required muscle power—pounding the rice into flour, grating the daikon, peeling chestnuts, or grinding sesame into paste—for the sight of her twisted, swollen fingers forcing their way into the dough hurt me. Then, as we worked together, she would tell me stories about the people in the village, and about Ryu's family. Okaa-san told me about Ryu's father and his grandmother who had been a famous singer and how they had always fought so loudly that the entire village could hear them, or the village miser who died because he refused to be parted from his money which he hid in his mattress and couldn't pull out in time when his house caught fire. She was a great storyteller and somehow always managed to make even the darkest stories funny. I often thought of confiding in her, for the weight of unsaid words sat heavy on my heart. But I knew that she wouldn't understand and I didn't want to see distance creep into her eyes. So I just let her talk and one day the thought came to me that maybe even my story had a funny side. In the afternoons, I read, or just sat and stared at the garden, watching the light change and tracking the many different sorts of movements of the plants, till it was time to meet Okaa-san in the kitchen again.

Unlike Okaa-san, her husband, the priest, hardly spoke at all. Even to his wife or to those that came to him for advice, he said only what was necessary. But a man doesn't have to speak for a woman to grow fond of him. At first I avoided him and he me. Then one day he found me sitting in a corner of the garden. We looked at each other for a long moment and

I felt him reach into my soul. Then he turned and left me alone. After he left I felt bad, as if I had been tested and found wanting. A few days later he came up to me with a clipper and said, "Come." I took the implement and followed him. He led me to a momiji tree and indicated where I should cut. "This one is old. Cut all that is unnecessary and leave only what is necessary for the tree to survive," he ordered.

"But how am I to know what is necessary and what is not?" I wanted to ask since I was no gardener. But his back was already turned and I knew I would get no answer. So I looked at the tree instead and tried to imagine what the tree would need to survive the winter. Very little, I realised in amazement, and knew I had my answer.

I took the cutter and began cutting away the longest branches, those that I thought would be most likely to break under the weight of the snow. I also cut away the few leaves that were left, for they stopped the tree from falling asleep properly. I was so involved in imagining the tree's life that I didn't hear the priest approach.

"That is good," he said, giving me one of his rare smiles.

They say an addiction is hard to cure. But while I was living with Okaa-san, I hardly ever missed the shops. In the beginning, in the middle of the night sometimes, the urge to buy would bite me and I would curse Ryu and think of the worst things I could to say to him when he returned. But as the days passed, this happened less and less. Sometimes I missed the children or Ryu but since he called the house every weekend it was all right, the missing never turned into worry. After Ryu, the children spoke to me but they said even less than their father. But however little they said, it felt good to hear them. Even the sound of their breathing was so familiar and I looked forward to being close to them again. Ryu's

195

mother never spoke to me but I knew she was there, for every once in a while I heard a noise in the background, a quickly smothered laugh or dishes being washed noisily somewhere. In the beginning, each time he called, I would ask Ryu when he would come to get me. He always said soon, soon but never gave me a date. So when January came, I stopped asking.

I hope you don't mind that I am taking so long with my story. But I want you to understand that I am not all that bad. When I was living in that house, surrounded by a Japan I had never seen before, I became another person. Even my body felt different—bigger and more supple—as if space had entered all the joints, softening them. The hole inside me like a crying mouth was filled—with what I do not know, good food, good air, new thoughts perhaps—and I felt at peace. I was no longer a black shadow, I had substance and weight. I too grew roots in the garden.

I wish I could show it to you, that garden. When I die I would like my remains to be buried in it so that my bones and my ashes can experience the beauty of the seasons year after year in that place. And with time, maybe the roots of the trees would become my arms and the sacred spring would cleanse my soul and fresh soft moss would become my skin and my hair.

But in the New Year, at the end of February when the snow began to melt, Ryu came back.

I can still remember the day so well. I was sitting in a patch of sunshine, looking out at the snow-covered garden. The only thing that moved was the water and even this seemed to have slowed down, moving lethargically, a fat black snake in a white landscape. I felt my body grow still and quiet as a rock. My thoughts slowed down and had almost disappeared entirely when Ryu's hand fell on my shoulder. I was so startled

I nearly fell off the wooden platform. No-one had touched me in months and suddenly there was Ryu's hand, so alien, yet warm and alive, resting heavily on me. He sat down beside me, still smelling of the airplane. "You've become fatter," were his first words, "it suits you."

The words hit me like a bomb. For two months I had not considered how I looked, for there were no mirrors in the house except in the bathroom. I stood up quickly, my hands going to my naked face, devoid of make-up. "You should have told me you were coming," I said sharply. "I... I could have prepared myself better."

Ryu stood up too. He looked disappointed. "Aren't you happy to see me?" he asked.

Again, I was caught unawares.

"Of course I am but... but I could have looked better if you had told me." With my eyes I begged him to understand, but of course he didn't.

"You are still worried about how you look," he remarked, turning away from me to look at the garden.

Then Okaa-san arrived with hot tea and a plate of freshly made warabi mochi with brown sugar sauce. "Here you are, my dears," she said, putting the tray down. "I will go and see what I can make for your dinner."

We ate our mochi in silence, looking out at the quiet garden. Just as I was about to make my escape, Ryu spoke again.

"When I was a child, during my school vacations," he said, "my mother, who never took leave from work ever, brought me here and left me for the holidays." A wistful smile curled the corners of his thin, serious lips. "When I did something naughty, Otoo-san would scold me and sometimes he even beat me. But then Okaa-san made me warabi mochi and I felt better. Those were the happiest times of my life."

I knew he was trying to apologise but something hard had formed inside me. And me, I wanted to ask, when you licked my breasts till the nipples became raw, did I not make you happy?

The next day we returned to Tokyo.

The City of Giants

Hard as it was to say goodbye to Okaa-san, it was even harder to say goodbye to the garden. The morning of our departure, when my eyes opened, I felt a heaviness in my chest, as if something were about to be pulled out. I slipped through the shoji and went outside. It was not yet 6 a.m. but the sky was a clear soft blue tinged with purple and I could tell it was going to be a beautiful day. Soon the snow would sparkle in the sun like a million diamonds or like fireworks going off against a milky sky. But the sun hadn't arrived yet and so the snow itself looked sleepy and unmoving, with a slight blue tinge. The trees and rocks were like black wounds in the snow, oozing the coldness of the night.

Barefoot, I walked across the unmarked snow to the water's edge. Under the snow, moss tickled my feet, springy and surprisingly alive. The only sound that could be heard was that of slowly trickling water. But even this had a sleepy muffled feel to it. How will I survive in Tokyo, I asked the water. What I meant of course was how would I survive without the garden to restore balance in my wayward heart? Then I heard a sound, a strange hollow tapping sound. I had never heard anything like it before and I looked up instinctively, knowing somehow that it was coming from the trees.

And then I saw it. Just above my head, not three feet above, on the branches of the momiji I had myself cut and prepared for the winter, upside down on the branch, was a bird. It was black on the top with four white dots on each of the wingtips, a bright red bottom and a black and white and red head. I stared at the bird in amazement. It was the first bird I had ever seen so close, the first real bird, I mean. Of course I had seen pigeons and crows and things in the city. But this bird was different. It was a real bird and felt different somehow, as if it neither hated nor loved me but was content to share its space with me. And the colours! And the pattern! No fashion designer could have ever designed a dress which looked so good. The bird turned suddenly and I caught sight of its belly which was the palest of browns mixed with a touch of grey and some beige. I had never ever in my life seen a colour like it, for just looking at it I could feel the soft warmth and the coziness of it. At the bottom was the red again, so alive and confident, and yet serving only to highlight the gentleness of the other colour. Then the bird moved again and I became aware of the strength of the creature, how its beak hit the hard wood relentlessly in search of food. The white snow-covered stillness made a perfect foil for its small but strong movements and I felt suddenly certain that if the bird could survive such hard winters without food, I too could survive Tokyo.

Something happened to me then, something I have difficulty describing. It entered me through my toes, passing through the soles of my feet, my ankles, my legs. I stood absolutely still and yet every part of me was on fire and dancing. Never in my life have I felt so alive, not even when I have just finished shopping. I stood there until the bird flew away. I could no longer feel my legs but I felt connected to the earth in a way that I have never felt since. Carefully I retraced my footsteps, walking backwards so as to preserve the marks I'd made in the snow. I hoped the garden would remember me even after my footsteps had disappeared.

Everything went very fast after that. When I returned, Ryu was waiting for me. We said goodbye to Okaa-san and Otoo-san who blessed us, and after that I remember very little till we got out of the airport at Haneda. It was as if, in the time I had been away, someone had come and subtly changed the proportions of the city I had so loved, making the buildings too big and tall and the roads too broad so that it was no longer a city for people but a city for giants.

Except that the giants had not come. Instead, there were only humans, small and lost in the vastness of what they had created. At the same time I couldn't help but notice how elegant the women were in their high heels and well-cut coats... and how the men too were so well-dressed. The expensive clothes certainly made them seem bigger and stronger than country folk, almost as if they were in fact a superior race. But when you looked into their faces, something was missing—as if their spirits were elsewhere, waiting for their bodies to catch up.

The second shock came when we boarded the metro and instead of going south we took the Keihin Tohoku line going north.

"What... where are we going?" I asked Ryu hesitantly.

"Home," he said calmly. But his face betrayed him.

"What do you mean? We don't live in the north. Are you joking?" I demanded loudly. Ryu looked around embarrassed but no-one was looking at us.

"I forgot to tell you. We've moved." At first I could think of nothing to say.

Then I said, accusingly, "You sold the house without telling me."

"Umm. I got a good deal," he answered vaguely. Then, "You always said you wanted to live in Tokyo and not in the suburbs." But for me Tokyo was Omotesando and Roppongi and Ginza. We got off the train at Oji station way up in the north. My first impression was that I had walked onto a 1960s film set, for there was something hasty and unfinished about the place. Yet there, just above the simple two-storey houses and shops, was the highway and the Shinkansen line on its raised concrete pillars.

Around the station, apart from the convenience store and the pachinko parlours, the buildings were all old and tired looking, and even those that weren't old managed to seem dirty and tired like their neighbours. In contrast, the colours on the billboards were vulgar and too bright. Three streets branched out from the front of the station, one was a shopping street and the other two meandered into a densely packed cluster of houses. It was all depressingly familiar, reminding me of the cheap, working-class neighbourhoods I had lived in as a child. I turned to Ryu, begging him with my eyes to tell me it was all a mistake, a joke. But, instead, he turned away and walked swiftly down the road to the left of the station. "Follow me," he said over his shoulder, "it's not far."

We walked down a shopping street full of messy, old-fashioned mom and pop stores selling everything from used televisions and dishwashers to paint, electric wires and cheap underwear. Everything was cheap and ugly and spoke of a life spent watching every yen. After a few minutes we rejoined the railway tracks, walking alongside them for about half a kilometre until we came to a stairway that allowed us to cross to the other side. At the top of the stairs I got my first view of my new neighbourhood: a sea of two-storeyed houses with identical roofs. "You'll be happy to know, this is a very safe neighbourhood," Ryu remarked, putting his hand on my shoulder. "That large building there is the Self-Defence forces' property." I looked across the roofs to where his finger pointed. There was a large sports ground right beside it but otherwise the grey cement four-storeyed building it was indistinguishable from any other government school or hospital building.

"What is that over there?" I pointed to dense knot of green on top of a cliff.

"That must be Asukayama park," he said, crinkling his eyes as he looked westwards into the setting sun. "This is a really Japanese neighbourhood you know, no foreigners here," Ryu said proudly. "But you have everything you need, the middle and high-schools over there are brand new, and we have two hospitals within easy reach and an old-age centre. All very convenient."

I looked at the modest little houses and imagined their cramped, dark interiors. None had a garden; it was a strictly working-class neighbourhood. All of a sudden, a giant hand grabbed my chest and began to squeeze all the air out of it. I held on to the railing in front of me feeling as if I would faint.

"Are you all right?" Ryu asked. He sounded really concerned, but I could not see him. There was only grey in front of my eyes.

"Yes, I'm fine," I replied weakly.

Ryu helped me down the stairs. At the bottom, we crossed the street, turned immediately to the right and entered a narrow little residential lane. I held on to my husband tightly, scared of getting lost. A memory from my childhood hit me suddenly with such force that I stopped. A very old man walking carefully across the street in just such a neighbourhood as the one I was now in. He had been bent almost double over his cane and I could clearly see the parchment texture of his skin, and the yellow of his eyes. And I remembered how I had felt hatred rise up inside me at his age and ugliness, and fear that one day I would be the same. The memory came wrapped in a scent, the scent of mothballs. Except the scent was real, escaping discreetly from every house that we passed. I stopped short. I didn't want the scent to catch me, I didn't want to smell of mothballs and be old. But even as I denied it, I knew that old age had finally found me, and it would never let me go.

"Hurry up, we're almost there," Ryu said impatiently.

I forced my feet forward, conscious of eyes watching us from behind curtained windows.

At last, Ryu stopped in front of a house. It was much smaller than our old house and it looked just like all the other houses we'd passed, a little smaller perhaps and a little newer, but otherwise the same. On the ground floor there was an entrance and a covered parking. Our old Honda was in it and I felt so happy to see it there that I almost went and kissed it. Ryu opened the front door and waited for me to enter. I hesitated. This was not my house, someone had made a terrible mistake. I could never call such a miserable ugly house my home.

The first thing I noticed was the furniture. "What did you do with our things?" I asked.

"What things?" Ryu frowned. "You mean the furniture? I sold it with the house. And got a good price too because the wife of the man who bought it liked the stuff so much. It would have cost more than what I paid for this stuff to have it brought over and wouldn't have fit in here, not to mention making the neighbours jealous. With the money they gave me I bought us this new stuff. I thought we should have a new life."

Except that the place he'd chosen for our new life was old and dirty and moth-eaten, and the furniture was second-hand.

Another terrible thought came to me and I rushed up the narrow stairway to the bedrooms. There were three doors, I pushed one open at random. Immediately I saw the computer and the ninja posters and realised it was the wrong room. I opened the other two doors and on my last try entered our bedroom. The cupboard was small, half the size of our old one, and so was the room. I was staring into it looking for my things when Ryu entered behind me.

"Are you looking for your clothes?" he asked quietly.

I turned to him angrily. "Where are they?" I demanded.

"You had so much stuff, we didn't know what to do with it, so mother packed what she could and sold the rest."

"What? You let her sell my things without asking?" I screamed.

"We couldn't help it. You can see there isn't enough place for all your stuff in such a small house," Ryu answered, backing away from me. He had on his banker's face, smooth and deceptive as a sheet of blank paper. It was the face I most hated and my hand itched to slap it. Those clothes were my friends, I wanted to shout, how dare he throw them away? But I knew he would not understand and so I bit back my anger and said instead, "I'm thirsty," and headed downstairs.

"There are some of your things in the cupboard in front of the bathroom and more in a suitcase downstairs in the basement," he called after me. I didn't answer, feeling as if I had betrayed my pets.

"And my shoes? Where did you put them?"

"In the basement," came the reply.

I felt indignant. What kind of peasant fool puts Prada and Ferragamo shoes in a basement? But before I could go and rescue them, on the table in the middle of the kitchen another surprise, a white, official-looking envelope with my name on it, awaited me. Seeing that it was from my bank, I opened it hurriedly. It was a letter from the bank stating that since we were leaving Tokyo, on my husband's request, my account had been closed and the money in the account had been sent to my husband's account. I was still staring at it, feeling as if the sky had fallen down on me, when Ryu called to me. "Kayo-chan, come here, I have something for you."

I ran upstairs to the bedroom, in search of an explanation. He was lying in the bed, naked. On the futon cover was a synthetic black lace bra with matching underwear, the kind of thing cheap prostitutes wore. I looked at it uncomprehendingly.

"Put it on," he said. Under the futon I saw his hand moving rhythmically up and down. "Come on, quickly now."

Still I did nothing, some part of me refusing to accept what was to come. If I had been smart I would have laughed and said, "Not now, I have my period" or something. But, instead, I just stood there looking stupid.

"Come on, you know what to do," Ryu said hoarsely. "You've done this many times before. You're a pro, aren't you? Do you want me to pay you, eh?"

Then I understood. Who was it that had told him? I didn't have to look far for an answer. It had to be the mother. She had always disapproved of me, hated me even.

As if I were in a dream, I began to take off my clothes one by one. When I was naked I tried to get inside the bed but he kicked me in the stomach.

"Put them on. I want to see if I got the right size."

"It's cold. Please, Ryu-chan, stop it. I'm sorry, I'll never do it again. I promise. I was sick then but I am well now," I begged him.

"You may be well now, but you haven't yet been punished," he said calmly.

It was then that I realised he was serious and so there was

only one thing for me to do—run out of the house. But he saw me backing away, reaching for the door, and quick as lightning he grabbed me, threw me onto the bed on my stomach and climbed on top of me. Then he took my panty and stuffed it into my mouth and made a gag for me using my T-shirt. Then, sitting astride my thighs, he used my stockings to tie my hands to the bed. Then he grabbed my legs and forced them apart. He put his hand roughly inside me, hurting me deliberately.

"Is this what they did to you, those men? Is this how you liked it?" he asked.

I struggled and kicked like a demon but I could not get him off me. The gag was choking me. I could smell my own juices on the underwear and their woman scent made me feel sick with rage and sadness.

And then came the most horrible moment of my life. I felt the cheeks of my buttocks being pushed apart and Ryu ramming himself inside, again and again and again. I felt something tear inside me and pain like lightning went through me all the way up into my lower back. At the same time, something hot and wet began to fall onto my back, growing cold as the tears formed a puddle in the small of my back. It took me a while to realise what the coldness was. Ryu had been crying. We had both been crying.

When it was over, Ryu got a towel and stanched the blood flowing out of me. Then he untied me and left the room. I heard him enter the bathroom and the shower being switched on.

I crawled under the covers of the futon and wished I was dead. But what got me up was the sound of the children's voices crying, "Mama, Mama, is she here? Has she come back?" from downstairs.

"Yes, wait a minute, she is in the bathroom," I heard Ryu reply.

I stumbled into the bathroom. Ryu had left the shower running and I got under it thankfully. He had also, strangely enough, filled the tub with hot water, and so after I had showered I got inside and let the heat soak into my aching body. In a few minutes my pain went away, but I still felt dirty. Something inside me was broken. I could feel it. I felt angry too, but it wasn't an active sort of anger. It was the kind that sat like a stone inside the stomach and wouldn't move.

"Mama, mama. Hurry and come out. We have a surprise for you," I heard Haruka say from the other side of the door. Reluctantly, I got out of the bathtub and put on a bathrobe.

The children were waiting for me on the other side and as soon as I opened the door they threw themselves into my arms, swamping me with their caresses. I held on to them tightly and the tears I had been holding back for so long began to flow freely out of my eyes. I felt the stone inside me shift a little but when I saw Ryu in the corridor looking at us, a beer in his hand, the stone slid back into place.

All the way till dinner, Akira and Haruka hovered over me, talking and asking questions in one and the same breath. Akira complained that his papa was a terrible cook, and grandma a dreadful housekeeper. Haruka wanted to tell me all about school and some sports team she had been elected to. I drank in the sound of their young voices, so different from the voices of the old ones in Kyushu. In the dark cramped kitchen of the new house, where the scent of mothballs and bad drains met and married, I began to prepare dinner, remembering with regret the large old-fashioned kitchen in Kyushu with the tofu and daikon tied up in straw and drying on wall and Okaa-san's leathery voice telling stories of the other world. As I was cutting the cucumber, a thought came to me which made me stop what I was doing. My family was my garden,

I realised, the only one that mattered. And so, in spite of the pain and the humiliation, I managed to make dinner a happy event. Everyone remarked on how good my cooking was and we talked and laughed as we hadn't done in ages. Even Ryu suddenly talked, making us laugh with a story about the local butcher and his five aged and smelly dogs. I looked at him in surprise, he seemed so normal and gentle, so much the Ryu I had always known that I could hardly believe that just a little while earlier he had done what he had done to me. Then Akira told another story about the local Takarazuka girls who kept trying to make him join them and we all laughed long and hard.

Dogenzaka Shadows

If only things had remained the way they were that first evening I could perhaps have forgiven Ryu for what he had done to me. I was, in spite of everything, happy to be with my children again. For children are the bits of a woman's heart that are placed in a new body and set free. Only when she is reunited with her children can a mother know peace.

But nothing remains the same—except clothes. That is why I love clothes so much. If you have clothes you don't need friends or even family. Within days the children had forgotten that I had ever gone away. Haruka, because she had been selected for the school swimming team, now spent all day and part of the weekends at school. When she came home it was only to change, to eat and then sit by herself in her room and talk to her friends. Akira was silent but once he felt reassured that I wasn't going away again, he stopped following me around the house and behaved as he had always done, locking himself up inside his room with his computer the moment he came back from school. Ryu went to work the next morning and though his office was quite close, in Shinjuku, he never came home before 10 p.m.

I tried to concentrate on the house, to brighten it up and give it a more modern feel. But there was nothing to be done with the dark little rooms and Ryu wouldn't hear of changing the old-fashioned wallpaper. Nor would he consent to throwing away the grey and mustard sofas he'd bought. And since no sunlight ever entered and Ryu would not hear of changing the fluorescent tubelights for more expensive yellow lights, I could not fight the darkness either.

So I decided to spring clean the house. I began at the top with Haruka's room, then Akira's and then ours. It was a difficult task, for though they had only been inside for a few weeks, their rooms looked as if they had been lived in for months. When I finished with the second floor, I moved down to the first floor. The living area was easily done but the kitchen took a very long time as years of grease had to be doggedly scraped off.

After around two weeks of very hard labour, when there was nothing left to do, I went down to the storeroom in the basement where the suitcases which held my clothes were.

As I have already said, clothes are like pets. If they are not looked after and petted every day, they grow sad and age quickly. When I opened the suitcases in the basement I could not recognize my beautiful expensive playthings in those sad, crumpled, evil-smelling rags. For apart from being dark, the basement was also very moist and some of the clothes had grown fungus on them. But to my surprise I felt nothing for those sad ruined clothes except a faint disgust. They didn't feel like my things. For me, and this is a truth every woman will agree with, clothes belong to those who desire them, and that is why women must keep running back to shops, for only shops know, as do women, that clothes are really truly beautiful only before they are bought. I quickly put the clothes into garbage bags and threw them away.

A year passed in the new house. I began to get used to the old-fashioned neighbourhood. The house was just the place I slept and ate in and the streets were where I did my shopping. But what I did notice at least in the beginning was that everyone in the neighbourhood looked old—even the children. No-one wore bright colours or fashionable clothes. Not even the young girls. When the women went shopping, they wore aprons and often the old men simply walked out in their pajamas. But soon I ceased to notice or be amazed. When I shopped, I wore an apron too and sensible shoes that cost only two thousand yen and weren't even leather. I didn't go to hairdressers any more, for the ones in my neighbourhood were useless. Instead, I let my hair grow long and tied it in a ponytail. Neither did I go to the drug store or to the convenience store, so I had no idea what the latest fashion was. Instead, I bought my vegetables in the market nearby and my meat at the local butcher's (the same one with the five smelly dogs), and my tofu at the old tofu shop run by the ninety-year-old woman. For the other things, I sent Akira out so that I would not be tempted.

Once, out of curiosity, I went to the Asukayama park nearby. It was big and dense and the paths were filled with old people on walkers or mothers with babies. Even the trees looked different, planted with no real thought towards aesthetics. Nothing in the vegetation even remotely reminded me of the garden in Kyushu. For there was no grand design to the park, I realised. It was just a collection of paths weaving in and out of trees. When I returned to the house, I burst into tears. And when the tears finally stopped, I realised that I felt different, smaller and somehow, heavier.

A month before the New Year, I asked Ryu timidly what his plans for the New Year were. Normally, either we went to Kita-Kyushu or his mother came to us. But I could not bear the idea of seeing his mother after all that she had done to me. For I was sure that it had been her idea to move to

213

this neighbourhood and that she had chosen the house. Only someone like my mother-in-law could have chosen such an ugly place, I knew, for she was the kind of person for whom a house was like a locker in a train station, just a place to park one's things. All that mattered to her was money.

"My plans?" Ryu looked up from his newspaper. "I don't know. Why? Is there something you would like to do?"

I felt surprised. It was the first time he had ever asked me what I would like to do. "I don't know, it's just so boring to always do the same thing," I said finally. "What I don't want to do is go to your mother's."

I don't know what made me say it, but across the room I could feel Ryu's body freeze.

Luckily, Haruka, who had come downstairs at that moment and had overheard the last part of our conversation, immediately ran to her father and said, "Yes, yes Papa, Mama is right. Let's not go to Kyushu, please. Kyushu is so old-fashioned. Let's go to Niigata instead. All my friends are going there. I want to ski."

"*Uhh*. I'll think about it," Ryu said, retreating behind his newspaper.

But a week later at dinner, he announced, "We will go to Echigo Yuzawa for one week during New Year."

The three of us were so surprised, we stopped eating and began to talk all at the same time. But of course I let the children speak and contented myself with smiling at Ryu whenever he looked my way. When they had run out of questions and Haruka had excused herself and gone up to her room to inform her friends, I asked Ryu, "How did you do it? Isn't it very expensive? Can we afford it?"

"Not if we were paying for it," Ryu replied, looking pleased with himself, "but we will be staying in a friend's flat. It is a super luxurious modern building with great views of the snow and an onsen and a restaurant even."

"But... what about skiing? The children and I don't ski. You haven't learnt to ski, have you?" I asked.

Ryu smiled, a strangely youthful smile. "Not yet, but I will learn. The children and I will take classes at my friend's school. He's promised to give us a hefty discount."

I nodded, not really able to picture them on skis. I didn't even notice he hadn't mentioned me till I remarked, "I have no ski clothes either—I'll have to buy some too."

Ryu replied immediately, "That won't be necessary. You can stay in the apartment and enjoy the onsen. Relax a bit."

I bit my lip, fighting back the angry words that were on the tip of my tongue. Then I asked, "When will we leave? I need to prepare things."

"On 29 December. You have two weeks. Better make sure we have lots of warm clothes."

It became really cold in Tokyo. A freezing wind rattled the naked branches of the trees in Asukayama park, and penetrated even the heaviest of coats, quickly numbing ears, noses and feet. The old stayed inside their homes and so did the mothers with young children. In our neighbourhood, the streets were empty and deserted even in the middle of the morning. On the news at night, they talked of finding frozen bodies under bridges and in parks, homeless men who never woke up to see the light of the new day. But when the wind finally stopped, heavy grey clouds rolled in, shutting out the light. One dark, icy day followed another, and we all retreated into ourselves. Meals became silent and no-one lingered at the table. The house was freezing cold and nothing I did seemed to make even the slightest bit of difference. The air-conditioners which were supposed to blow out hot air in winter didn't seem to remember that summer was over and continued to shoot ice-cold air at us. The kotatsu which I bought at a nearby store used so much power that we couldn't run any other appliances while it was on. There was nothing for any of us to do except retreat into our rooms straight after dinner and get inside our futons. By the end of the month, the days had grown indistinguishable from the nights and only the thought that soon we would be going on holiday stopped us from killing each other.

Then, the day before we left for Niigata, I woke up to find the sky was white and bright with snowflakes. At first I just stared at them in disbelief. It so rarely snowed in the city. Then a picture sprang into my mind, of a pure and pristine garden covered in snow and a brilliant black and white bird with flashes of red under its wings. I threw off the futon and rushed to the window. But the same grey roofs met my eyes, looking, if anything, a little uglier and greyer than before, for the snow melted as soon as it touched them. The same was true of the ground which was dirty grey or brown except for in those corners where the wind and the light never entered.

But at breakfast that day, Haruka's excitement was so great it infected all of us, even Akira. We spent the day packing and cross- checking lists. I began to feel excited too as the suitcases filled up the hallway. Dinner that night was a happy meal. Because Ryu had said he would be coming home for dinner, I had bought some beef and cooked shogayaki. This I heaped onto the fragrant new rice from Kyushu that Okaa-san had sent us that October. After dinner, instead of disappearing into our separate rooms, we all sat together, our legs entwined beneath the kotatsu, and watched the news and the second-last episode of the NHK drama *Mito Komon*.

I woke up very early the next morning. It was snowing

216

again. In the golden glow of the street lights, the snow sparkled like gemstones—giant sapphires and diamonds, rubies and pearls scattered carelessly on the ground. This time the snowflakes were so large and there were so many that I was sure they would stay. I was reminded of spring, of hanabira, the falling of cherry blossoms. Very quietly, so as not to disturb Ryu lying beside me, I began to hum a popular song from my teens, about lovers reunited under a cherry blossom shower. But since I could only remember the chorus, after I had sung it two or three times, I fell silent and simply watched them fall out of the sky.

The snow made everything feel calmer. It gave a purpose to the cold, a meaning other than simple punishment. Deep inside my body, where everything had been silent for so long, something moved. It was nothing more than a tiny flutter in my chest like a bird that had suddenly woken up after a long winter. But it made me shiver. I stared at the silently sparkling snow for a long time. For whom does the snow shine so brightly, I wondered. The answer of course was "no-one". Just shining and being beautiful was enough in itself. I got back into bed and inched my cold body closer to Ryu's, taking care, nonetheless, not to touch him. As my eyes closed again, I imagined the same snow falling in a garden somewhere in the hills of Kyushu.

When I awoke, Haruka was shouting in my ear, "Mama wake up, it is almost eight."

I sat up with a start, depriving Ryu of his share of the futon covering us both. Haruka was sitting on the bed, fully dressed.

I looked at the clock on the wall and saw that Haruka had lied, it was only 7.05 a.m.

"Go back to bed, or go read something," I said, annoyed.

"I can't, Mama." Haruka pouted. "Please hurry up and

get ready. Make us some breakfast quickly and then we can all get out of here. I am afraid that if we wait, the roads will get blocked."

She was right, so I sent her down to set the table for breakfast and shook Ryu awake. "It's snowing quite hard now," I told him as I headed for the toilet, "if we don't leave soon, the roads will be blocked."

When he heard that, Ryu was up in an instant. Down the corridor I could hear Haruka banging on Akira's door, demanding he wake up or be left behind.

I slipped into my clothes, shivering, as they touched my body. Outside, it was still snowing. Even in the grey morning light the snow looked clean and bright and pure. I had a strange thought: that the snow was like new clothes. The town put on the new clothes and became young and pure again.

The kitchen was still dark, but I switched on a tubelight and began to warm the rice, and reheat the vegetables on the stove.

Then I opened a tin of sardines and put them in a plate and took out the pickles from the fridge. Last of all, I made the soup. When everything was ready, I called for the others.

As always, Haruka came down first. She was followed closely by her father. Akira came last, a full five minutes later, still looking half-dressed. We sat down and ate without speaking but after a few moments I put down my chopsticks and watched them eat instead, my little family, my garden. Over their heads, my gaze extended to the window of the living area but I could see nothing except grey concrete wall. This spring, I decided, I would make a Japanese garden there between the wall and the house, a zen garden of my own. Once again, I saw an image of the garden in Kyushu, but this time it was not the back garden but the one in front of the temple, with the snow forming perfectly concentric circles around the stones. Otoo-san had explained to me that the snow or sand or gravel represented water, the sea, the symbol of life. "Draw those lines perfectly. It may look very simple but you need a completely still mind to do it. Even for a priest it is difficult." I begged him to let me try but he always refused, laughing it off.

"The sand has only one master, only one mind will it obey," he told me.

I was brought back to the present by Ryu saying severely, "This is not the time to dream. I am going to take the luggage out and pack it in the car. Can you be ready in fifteen minutes?"

I nodded and we all got to work. Haruka washed up while Akira and I made the beds and rolled up the futons. I looked at my checklist and tried to force my brain to think of what I had forgotten. Instead, my eyes kept going to the sparkling snow outside. How beautiful it was. How precious. It reminded me of the lights in Ginza on New Year's eve and the "Lucky Bag" sales on the first day of the new year. Suddenly, I longed to go there. I wanted to be a part of Tokyo once again. I wanted to walk amongst the well-dressed and happy throngs and think only of being happy once again. I don't know why these thoughts came to me just then. I pushed them away angrily, and tried to focus on the things I needed for the trip, but again my mind skittered away, presenting me with an image of Isetan's first-floor display windows on New Year's day. I shook my head and got rid of the image but not before I was hit by another pang of longing.

I forced myself to move, going from room to room, closing curtains, turning off lights. Predictably, Akira had forgotten his ski mask and goggles, so I picked them up and took them downstairs. I checked the windows in the kitchen and living room one last time, switched off the electricity and water and walked out, locking the door behind me.

Ryu had the engine running and the car was warm. But even before I had fully closed the door he began to drive.

"Wait a minute. Can't you let me get inside properly?" I cried. He wouldn't answer. Something inside me snapped. "You had no right to do that!" I said, grabbing his arm. The car swerved wildly, narrowly escaping the neighbour's electricity pole.

Ryu braked sharply. Then he turned and slapped me. No-one said anything for a minute. I opened the door of the car. "I forgot something," I mumbled, swinging my legs out of the car. Ryu grabbed my arm. "Leave it, you can buy whatever you need over there." I shook off his hand impatiently. "If you get out now, I won't wait for you," Ryu threatened. I got out and slammed the car door. "Mother, are you all right?" I heard Akira calling after me anxiously.

I didn't reply. It had begun to snow again. With each step my feet sank a few centimetres into the fresh snow. Why do we need to go to Niigata to see snow, I thought, when we have it right here in Tokyo? I stifled a giggle and walked back slowly up the street.

Behind me, Ryu honked impatiently. I pretended I hadn't heard. The sound of gears clashing and wheels rotating, wet, heavy snow flying and falling with a thud told me that they had gone. I opened the door and went inside. All that could be heard was the clock ticking above the kitchen table. Idly, I watched wet snowflakes chase each other down the windowpanes. I began to bet on which one would get to the bottom first. I had time. Lots of it. I knew they would not return. For, in reality, they did not need me. Haruka could cook for them.

After what seemed a long while I went upstairs to the bathroom. I looked at the mirror above the sink. It was an old mirror, a mirror with a history. Normally, I never looked at it because there was always someone else waiting to get into the bath or else, if I was the last one using it, I was too busy cleaning the bathroom. Now I scrutinized the mirror minutely. It was a strange mirror, not the usual plastic things that came with a prefabricated bathroom like this one. It had a wooden frame. And it hung at an angle. On the corner was an old sticker of Captain America. I looked at myself, framed by milky white light from the frosted-glass window. I could not see my features. All I could see was a smooth dark oval surrounded by brilliant white light. The flame had inverted itself. Now the darkness was inside and the light was a halo on the outside. But it felt right somehow. I felt light, lighter than I had felt in a long, long time. I took another look at my face but could still see nothing. I could have turned on the electric light, I suppose. But I had forgotten to turn the electricity on. So, instead, I peered once again at the darkness where my eyes, nose and lips should have been and this time I shivered. I left the bathroom hurriedly. Later, there would be time to examine my face in the mirror again—after I had gone out and bought myself some fresh make-up and smart clothes.

I wandered into the bedroom. The empty house felt strangely peaceful. I stood by the window and stared at the gnarled bark of the old cherry tree in our neighbour's garden. Soon spring would arrive and the cold would be defeated, I thought. One by one I began to take them off, the clothes I had bought for the ski holiday in Niigata. I took off the heavy second-hand down jacket and my Uniqlo jeans, the heavy Uniqlo sweater with the image of a reindeer galloping across the front. I took off the cotton turtleneck and my black tights. I was down to my underwear now but to my surprise I didn't feel cold. I twisted my hands to the back and took off my cheap synthetic 100 yen shop bra and then, bending, removed the sensible black and white spotted cotton panties, also from the 100 yen shop.

When I was completely naked, I opened the door and stepped onto the narrow balcony. I danced, I screamed abuses at the world, I used all the filthiest words I knew. I screamed Ryu's name. I screamed and screamed till I had no breath left in me. I didn't care if the neighbours heard. I wanted them to hear, to know what I thought of them. But no-one came outside, for it had begun to snow again. And even if they had come, they would have seen nothing.

For I had become invisible. As invisible as melted snow.

When I returned to my room, my clothes stared at me reproachfully. I looked at them in distaste. I knew where I had to go and what I would do. The lights of Ginza danced before my eyes. I put on those ugly sensible clothes for the last time.

You look at me incredulously. You don't believe me? You think because I am lying here beside you that I am being untruthful. But have you never wondered why it is that I never removed all my clothes? And why I insisted on absolute darkness? Maybe you thought it was because I could only be free and uninhibited in the dark. But that was never the case. In reality it is because I am cursed. I exist only when I have at least one brand-new piece of clothing on my body.

Don't try to move too much, for the poison will only kill you faster. It will not be long, a few hours at most. And I will not leave you till the end, I promise. I will not let you die alone. I already told the reception we would be staying all day. I will stay with you till your spirit leaves your body and when I leave this hotel I will look up at the night sky and imagine you there looking down at me. Free.

Do you believe in God? I am sure you don't. I am not sure I do either. But if there is such a thing as God, that God must be an old woman with wrinkled hands. Yes, wrinkled hands because she spends her day washing dirty old souls. I like to believe that just as the women who worked in this neighbourhood's old bath houses, cleaning and massaging clients' bodies, and for a little extra, even cleaning their ears, God cleans the souls that come to him and makes them new and pure again. Soon you will know. Your spirit too will go to a place where all the dirty creases in its used and wrinkled surface will be cleaned and then you will come back to this world in a new body.

There is a little flicker of movement in your cheek. You like what I say? You agree with me? How sad that you will never be able to speak again. I never wanted to kill you. You should not have asked me to tell you about myself. Other people's secrets are always dangerous. For a secret is only a secret when it is locked inside a single heart. But a time comes in a person's life when it is no longer possible to keep everything inside one self. So I told you my story. I thought my death would be enough. But as the secrets poured out of me, I realised that you would have to die too. For, you see, my story is not my story alone. It is the story of my club, and also of my country. It is the story of our shame.

You shake your head but I think you believe me a little. I think you have seen it too. Tokyo is beautiful. Tokyo is a forest of beautiful things. And it is so easy to want beautiful things. How can wanting to be happy be wrong? How can wanting to have beautiful things be wrong? But Happyism trapped us. And now we are only alive as long as we keep buying. That is why you must die. For no foreigner can know our secret and live. I could not be a traitor to my countrymen even in death.

Another five minutes and it will be over. Then I will clean the room, make the bed and shower you. And after I dry you and lay you out on the bed, I will dress you. I will turn down the heat so you will not smell when you are found and I will leave you to sleep. I like to be neat, you see. I like there to be neatness in everything I do. But especially I like to be neat around the dead. Out of respect.

Then I will undress myself and put my designer clothes in a plastic bag. I will take a bath and purify myself. Then I will dry myself with one of the hotel's nice fluffy towels and dust my face and arms with white powder. Then I will put on a second-hand white wedding kimono like the one I wore when I was married. White is also the colour of sacrifice, the colour of those samurai warriors who chose to die of their own hand rather than accept the shame of surrender.

I will go down the corridor noiselessly and throw the clothes into the garbage bin in the service area. Then I will take the stairs to the first floor, walk past the reception where the bored young girl with strawberry-coloured hair sits. I like the girl. She is from Aichi prefecture, and has been in Tokyo for barely two years. Her square peasant hands have nails painted in the latest fashion, animal prints in multi-colours with four Swarovski crystals on the outer edge of the nail. The t-shirt she wears is Dolce & Gabbana and under her desk is a pink plastic Louis Vuitton. She will never go back to her village, even though in this city she will never find a husband. I remember her when she started working at the hotel, all pink-cheeked and polite. Maybe I should tell her to go home, to leave this stinking lotus pond of a city alone. I am sure she has no husband, or even boyfriend, yet.

Maybe she will look up if I touch her face, my touch awakening some long-forgotten memory—of a beloved grandmother or an aunt, and it will make her smile. And in that fleeting moment she will be transformed into a simple young peasant girl again. But almost immediately she will control herself, shake her pink hair and frown at her nails. For she cannot see me.

And so I will smile at her in farewell and leave her to her fate. I will walk out of the front door onto the quiet Dogenzaka side-street, alone and free, and spend what remains of the night walking amongst my children. They are Dogenzaka's shadows and amongst them I will remain till the first morning train arrives to take me away.

About the Author

Ferrante Ferranti

Rhadika Jha is an Indian writer. She studied anthropology at Amherst College and did her Master's in Political Science at the University of Chicago. She has worked for *Hindustan Times* and *BusinessWorld*, as well as the Rajiv Gandhi Foundation, where she started up the Interact project for the education of the children of victims of terrorism in different parts of India. She regularly contributes to anthologies and her stories are published in newspapers and magazines. She has just moved to Beijing after living for six years in Tokyo with her husband and two children.